Lily Speaks!

Other Books Available

The Lily Series
 Here's Lily!
 Lily Robbins, M.D. (Medical Dabbler)
 Lily and the Creep
 Lily's Ultimate Party
 Ask Lily
 Lily the Rebel
 Lights, Action, Lily!
 Lily Rules!
 Rough & Rugged Lily
 Lily Speaks!
 Horse Crazy Lily
 Lily's Church Camp Adventure
 Lily's in London?!
 Lily's Passport to Paris

Nonfiction
 The Beauty Book
 The Body Book
 The Buddy Book
 The Best Bash Book
 The Blurry Rules Book
 The It's MY Life Book
 The Creativity Book
 The Uniquely Me Book
 The Year 'Round Holiday Book
 The Values & Virtues Book
 The Fun-Finder Book
 The Walk-the-Walk Book
 NIV Young Women of Faith Bible

Lily Speaks!

Nancy Rue

ZONDERVAN.com/
AUTHORTRACKER
follow your favorite authors

ZONDERKIDZ

Lily Speaks!
Copyright © 2002 by Women of Faith

Requests for information should be addressed to:

Zonderkidz, *Grand Rapids, Michigan 49530*

ISBN 978-0-310-70262-7

All Scripture quotations unless otherwise noted are taken from the *Holy Bible, New International Version*®. NIV®. Copyright © 1973, 1978, 1984 by International Bible Society. Used by permission of Zondervan. All rights reserved.

Published in association with the literary agency of Alive Communications, Inc., 7680 Goddard Street, Suite 200, Colorado Springs, CO 80920. www.alivecommunications.com

Zonderkidz is a trademark of Zondervan.

Editor: Barbara J. Scott
Interior design: Amy Langeler
Cover design: Jody Langley
Cover illustrator: Laura Tallardy

Printed in the United States of America

10 11 12 13 14 15 16 17 18 19 20 /DCI/ 30 29 28 27 26 25 24 23 22 21 20 19 18 17 16 15

Chapter 1

"The next time someone tells you to 'amscray,' 'go chase yourself,' or 'come clean,'" Lily Robbins said to her class, "you'll know exactly what to do. Slang changes, but people never do."

She let out a long, slow breath and forced herself not to go running back to her seat so she could melt into a puddle of relief. Mrs. Reinhold had said to pause at the end of the speech to maintain poise—or something. Right now, Lily was more interested in maintaining her dignity. *I really should've gone to the bathroom before she called on me,* she thought.

But if anyone noticed that Lily was dying to get away from the podium, they weren't showing it. The seventh-grade accelerated English class burst into applause. There were even a few whistles thrown in, which Lily was sure were coming from her best friend, Reni. Still, it wasn't a bad feeling having everybody cheer. It almost made the pre-speech agony worthwhile.

"Thank you, Lilianna," Mrs. Reinhold said in her cobwebby voice. "Here is your outline. All right—next—oh, in fact, last—we will hear from Suzanne Wheeler."

Lily took her outline from Mrs. Reinhold, but her eyes went to Suzy—her other closest friend. Lily had been terrified to give her first middle-school speech, so she knew Suzy was probably about to throw up. Suzy got nervous when she had to open a milk carton with people watching. Lily had told the other Girlz—Reni, Kresha, and Zooey—just that morning that she wasn't sure Suzy could make it through a whole speech.

Lily sank into her seat, still zoning in on Suzy, who finally looked at her. Lily gave her a firm nod.

You can do this, girl, it said. *We prayed and everything this morning. You can do this.*

For an instant, Suzy's fragile black eyebrows relaxed from the knot they were tied in, and a small smile eased across her lips.

"You go, girl," Lily whispered.

Suzy gave the tiniest of nods, barely stirring a strand of her silky dark hair. Then she took a deep breath, gazed out at the class, and began to talk.

For the first few words, her voice was faint, and Lily had to squeeze her hands together to keep from calling out, "Speak up, Suzy!" Mrs. Reinhold had gone on for almost a whole class period about what she was going to do if she couldn't hear somebody. Something about cupping her hand around her ear and saying, "Eh?"

But suddenly Suzy's voice went up a few notches and began to sound warm. Her hands relaxed on the sides of the podium so that her knuckles were no longer white, and she looked around at the class as she spoke with her eyes shining. Not once did Lily see her glance down at her copy of the outline. If Lily hadn't known better, she'd have thought Suzy was enjoying herself up there.

I sure didn't, Lily thought. *I was scared to death the entire time.*

When Suzy closed with her last line, the class broke into applause before Suzy could even do her pause. Her little face lit up, and she cocked her head to one side, splashing her hair against her cheek. That seemed to make the class clap even louder.

Lily was right in there clapping with them, although for just a moment, she couldn't help thinking it would be nice to have hair like Suzy's. Lily's mane was red and curly and wouldn't splash against her cheek if it were soaking wet. Suzy really was fun to look at.

"Well, then," Mrs. Reinhold said as she closed her grade book and came up the aisle to the front of the room. "This was not bad for a first round of speeches. Not bad at all."

That was high praise coming from strict, stone-faced Mrs. Reinhold, and it gave Lily the courage to look at her outline.

A. Very nice work, Mrs. Reinhold had written. Lily let out another sigh of relief.

"Would you hold it down, Robbins?" Ashley Adamson hissed from the seat in front of Lily. "You sound like a bus back there."
Lily did what she'd learned was best to do when it came to Ashley — ignore her.

"Now," Mrs. Reinhold was saying. "I didn't tell you this before we started giving our speeches because some of you were already biting your fingernails up to your elbows." Lily glanced down at her chewed-up nails and quickly slid her hands under her thighs.

"You have just competed in the first level of a speech contest," Mrs. Reinhold went on, "which is being held statewide for all seventh graders. Two of you will go on to compete with students from the other seventh-grade English classes for the school title, and the winner will go on to the county competition. One speaker from that tournament will go on to compete on the state level."

Marcie McCleary's hand went up.

"Yes?" Mrs. Reinhold said, her voice clipped.

"Is the state tournament out of town? Because if it is, I can't go. My parents won't let me go on school trips out of town."

"You don't need to concern yourself, Marcie," Mrs. Reinhold said. "You are not one of the two contestants I have selected from this round."

"Who are they?" Ashley said.

Is there no end to Ashley's cluelessness? Lily thought.

Mrs. Reinhold glared at Ashley and then said, "I believe that the two best speeches for this competition were given by Lilianna Robbins and Suzanne Wheeler. They will be our class representatives to the seventh-grade contest."

Lily could feel her mouth dropping open. It was all she could do to keep from standing up and shouting, *No way! I'll completely freak out!*

But to her surprise, the class had burst once again into applause. Ashley, of course, only slapped her hands together a few times before she busied herself looking in her pocket mirror, but everybody else kept it up for a good minute. Reni, Lily saw, was the last one to stop whistling and stomping her feet. Even after the clapping stopped, she grinned at Lily from across the room, her wonderful brown face shiny.

Lily grinned back and then looked around for Suzy. Her little dark-haired friend was staring at her desktop, face as white as a bowl of Cream of Wheat.

Yikes, Lily thought. *She doesn't want to do this. She's gonna die!*

Reni, who sat only one row over from Suzy, leaned across the aisle and shook Suzy's arm.

"You go, girl!" Reni said.

It was the last thing to be shouted before Mrs. Reinhold snapped them all to order again, but it seemed to perk Suzy up. Still, Lily couldn't shake the feeling that this was putting Suzy in a bad place—a really bad place.

It's a good thing we have Girlz Only this afternoon, Lily thought. *Maybe we can help her find a way to get out of it.*

Lily was composing the speech Suzy could give to Mrs. Reinhold, when Mrs. R. gave one more announcement.

"The school-wide seventh-grade speech contest will be one week from tonight, in the auditorium. You are all invited to come, and I think you will want to support your classmates."

Ashley raised her hand.

"Yes?" Mrs. Reinhold said.

"Who's in it from your other classes?" Ashley tossed her flipped-up blonde hair. A couple of pieces were displaced in the toss. Lily knew she'd have that mirror back out within thirty seconds.

"I will post a list tomorrow," Mrs. Reinhold said.

"Did Benjamin Weeks make it?"

"Look at the list tomorrow," Mrs. Reinhold said. "Now — your homework assignment — "

Ashley turned her head just a quarter of a turn so she could speak out of the side of her mouth to Lily without Mrs. Reinhold seeing.

"I bet Benjamin gets picked for first period," she said. "He's way good — you don't have a chance against him."

Lily could feel her eyes going into slits. She might be putting out sweat balls already at the thought of giving a formal speech from the podium in the auditorium, but the thought of possibly losing to Benjamin Weeks was even more revolting.

Besides, all the cheering and clapping on her behalf today had been pretty cool. Think how much of it there would be at a county contest — or even better, a state tournament.

The bell rang, jangling her back to the classroom. Ashley was the first one out the door, and Reni and Suzy appeared in her place.

"This is so awesome, you guys!" Reni said. "Two Girlz in the school contest. I'm jazzed!"

"I don't know if I am," Suzy said. "This is kind of scary."

Kresha and Zooey, the two other members of the Girlz Only Group, met them at the door, panting to know how everybody's speech had gone. All week they'd been the audience when Reni, Lily, and Suzy had

9

practiced. Like most things in their lives, if it was happening to one of them, it was happening to all of them. They were that close.

"Why did I know she was going to say that?" Reni said in a low voice to Lily as they fought their way down the crowded hall behind Kresha, Zooey, and Suzy.

"Say what?" Lily said.

" 'This is kind of scary,' " Reni said in a close imitation of Suzy's soft voice.

"Yeah, really," Lily said. "I'm kind of scared for her. She practically puked this time. What's she gonna do in front of all those people and parents and everything?"

Reni nodded thoughtfully, swinging her beaded braids back and forth. "But she did a good job on her speech," she said. "I was blown away."

"Me too," Lily said. "That was probably because we all helped her so much. We'll have to do the same thing for this contest."

"Yeah, but, Lil," Reni said.

She pressed her lips together as she looked at Lily, so that her dimples deepened in her cheeks.

"What?" Lily said.

"She's your competition now. You can't be helping her *too* much."

They'd reached fourth-period geography by then, and Ms. Ferringer was waiting to close the door. There was no time to argue the point with Reni, and Lily wasn't sure what she would have said anyway.

My competition? she kept thinking as she colored in the map of Asia. *That just doesn't feel right.*

Lily was still trying to get a grip on the competition thing when school was out that afternoon, and she headed for Zooey's house, which was only a few blocks from Cedar Hills Middle School. Zooey had a great basement, which her mom had redecorated as a meeting room for the Girlz Only Group's twice-weekly meetings. It was almost February, and Lily had to pick her way through gray slush to navigate the sidewalks without slipping, but her mind was almost completely on Suzy's problem as she walked, head down against the cold. So it surprised her when Zooey was suddenly in front of her, arms folded over her coatless chest, frosty air puffing out of her mouth.

"What are you doing out here without a coat?" Lily said. She glanced up at Zooey's house. "I know my way to the back door, Zo. You didn't have to come out and meet me."

"Yes, I did," Zooey said. She stamped her feet on the sidewalk and hugged herself tight. "I just want to make sure of something before Suzy gets here."

Lily glanced over her shoulder, but there was no sign of Suzy yet. "Make sure of what?" she said.

"Well—" Zooey's big, gray eyes rolled. Her little bow of a mouth was by now turning blue.

"Spit it out, Zooey!" Lily said. "I'm freezing, and I have a coat on. You have to be about to die—what's up?"

Zooey hunched herself closer to Lily and said in a low voice, "Don't make too much of a big deal about this speech contest thing. I don't want Suzy getting her feelings hurt."

"Why would I hurt Suzy's feelings?" Lily said. "I love Suzy!"

"Yeah, but you know how you are sometimes, Lily," Zooey said.

"No. How am I?"

"You know—you're the best at a lot of stuff, and you're always getting elected to stuff and getting to do cool things—and, like, Suzy got picked for this too, not just you."

Lily felt as if she'd been stung. She forgot the cold as she stared at Zooey.

"I know she got picked too," Lily said. "I haven't been bragging about how I'm gonna win or anything."

"I know," Zooey said hurriedly. "I just, like, didn't want you to start."

Lily opened her mouth to protest, but Zooey's eyes suddenly shifted over Lily's shoulder. "Suzy! Hi, sweetie!" she said. Then she engulfed Suzy in a huge hug and kept her arm around her as she led her to the house like she'd never been there before.

"That's okay," Lily muttered as she followed them. "I'll just walk by myself."

Zooey's mom had hot chocolate and popcorn ready for them, so the first couple of minutes were taken up with getting settled and chowing down. It took that long for Lily to shake the uneasy feeling she'd gotten when she talked to Zooey. It came right back as soon as Kresha brought up the subject again.

"I so proud of you, Su-zee and Lee-lee!" she said in her Croatian accent. When she was careful, she could sound more American, but right now she was excited. In fact, she seemed to be the most excited of any of them.

"You going to be vee-ners!" she said.

Zooey squeezed Suzy's hand. "I wish I coulda seen you do it for real. I bet you were incredible."

"She was great," Lily said, looking pointedly at Zooey.

Reni cleared her throat, but Lily shot her a warning look. After what Zooey had said, this wasn't the time to brag on Lily.

"I don't know," Suzy said. "I don't know if I can do this. I mean, the class is one thing, but there are going to be parents there." She giggled nervously. "*My* parents!"

Kresha and Zooey jumped in to squelch that kind of talk, which gave Reni and Lily a chance to have an eye conversation. As best friends, they could carry on an entire discussion without saying a word.

I don't think she can do it, Reni's eyes said.

Me neither, Lily's said back. *But don't say anything in front of her.*

Why?

I'll tell you later. But it has to do with Zooey.

Zooey gushed over Suzy for the rest of the meeting. By the time they had packed up their backpacks and put on their coats to go home, Suzy was beaming. For now, anyway, there didn't seem to be a nervous cell in her body.

"That's just for now," Reni said to Lily as they went down the sidewalk together. "Wait'll she gets in front of all those people. I've performed a lot in front of audiences, you know. It can totally freak you out — and I don't freak out that easy."

"Uh, Reni, could you cut it out?" Lily said. "Now you're freaking *me* out."

Reni let out a snort that sent frosty air spewing forth. "Are you kidding me?" she said. "You are so gonna win this, Lily. It's a piece of cake for you."

"But I've never really competed before," Lily said. "I don't know if I *can* win."

"Do you *want* to win?" Reni said.

Lily set her jaw. "I definitely want to beat Benjamin — if he's even in it."

"Okay, so here's how you do it," Reni said. "You practice more and work harder than anybody else. Period. That's how I always win first chair and got into All-State orchestra and all that."

Lily peeked at her from the confines of her pulled-tight knit cap. "You really think I could win?"

"You *so* could! Nobody talks better — or more — than you, Lil."

"Smack," Lily said without taking her hands out of her pockets.

"And don't worry about Suzy," Reni said. "Zooey's getting her all pumped up, but I'm on your side."

Reni took her hand out of her pocket long enough to give Lily's sleeve a squeeze. "See ya tomorrow," she said, and turned the corner to her street.

Lily walked the rest of the way home barely aware that a few snow-flakes were falling. All she could think about was Reni's last sentence: *I'm on your side.*

We don't take sides in Girlz Only Group, she thought. *Do we?* The next morning, she got her answer.

Zooey was the only one there when Lily arrived at the bench where the Girlz always met in the morning before school. She jumped up when she saw Lily and pounced on her before Lily could even get her backpack off.

"We have to talk before Suzy gets here!" Zooey said—instead of "Good morning" or even "Hi."

"We talked about this yesterday," Lily said as she slid her backpack off of her shoulders. "I did what you said at the meeting."

"I know," Zooey said. "But this is different. Lily—" She took a deep breath and straightened her shoulders. "I think you should drop out of the contest."

Lily froze with her backpack only halfway to the floor.

"For Suzy," Zooey said. "See—it's really bad that you two are competing against each other—"

"We're *not* really."

"And besides that, you always get to be in the spotlight and Suzy never does."

"But I'm not—"

"So I think you should be a good friend and let Suzy have a chance for a change."

Lily gave up trying to interrupt her. Besides, she had no idea what to say—except no. So she shook her head.

Zooey flung herself down on the bench and folded her arms. "Why not?" she said.

"Because." It was all Lily could get out. Everything was suddenly so tangled up inside, even her words were in a knot.

"Don't you even care about Suzy?" Zooey said.

"Yes!" Lily managed to say. "I was gonna help her with her speech—"

"You could help her more if you dropped out."

All Lily could do was shake her head, even when Zooey stomped her foot. Lily was sure Zooey would have thrown a full-out tantrum if she hadn't caught sight of Suzy coming down the steps from the locker area.

"I think you're being selfish, Lily," Zooey said between clenched teeth. And then she sprang up off the bench and met Suzy at the bottom of the steps.

Lily sat, completely confused.

I'm selfish? she thought. *Because I won't step down from a contest Suzy's too shy to win anyway?*

By then, Zooey and Suzy were at the bench, and Lily tried to act the way she would have if Zooey had never said a word. It was hard, though. Her smile felt as if it had been painted on with nail polish and left to harden.

"Morning, Suzy," she said. "Were your parents happy about the speech thing?"

"Uh-huh," Suzy said.

"Not as happy as I am," Zooey said. "Suzy, you are *so* gonna win. Have you picked out what you're gonna wear yet?"

Suzy shook her head.

"Okay—wow—I can help you there."

Zooey took Suzy by the arm and led her several steps from the bench and, leaning her head close to Suzy's, rattled on in tones Lily could barely hear. Lily could only stare at them. As aware as they seemed of her presence, she might as well have been watching them through a window.

When Kresha's voice bubbled over the hall noises, Lily had never been so glad to hear her. As soon as Kresha burst onto the scene and plopped down on the bench, she looked from Zooey and Suzy to Lily and scowled.

"Come over here, guys," she said. "We vant hear too."

Lily saw Zooey roll her eyes at Suzy before she answered.

"We were just talking about some stuff," she said.

"Vhat stuff?" Kresha said.

Please don't, Kresha, Lily wanted to say. *Don't make it worse.*

Although Lily didn't see how it could get much worse than two of her closest friends snubbing her. She felt as if she'd been punched in the stomach.

Fortunately, Kresha didn't wait for an answer to her question but stuck her hands in her coat pockets and pulled out what appeared to be two wads of tissue paper.

"I bring each a present," she said. "A con-gra-tu-la-tions present."

"Good word, Kresha," Suzy said. She was always Kresha's best cheerleader when it came to her learning new words in English.

I better say something nice about it too, Lily thought, *or Kresha's gonna be on Suzy's side.*

The minute the thought appeared in Lily's head it stunned her. *What am I saying? We don't take sides in Girlz Only!*

"Open!" Kresha said, pointing to the present she had dropped in Lily's lap.

Lily pulled back the tissue paper and discovered there was something inside: it was a tiny plastic skunk holding a sign that said "Good job!" She looked over to see Suzy pulling an identical one out of her paper.

"It is pen," Kresha said, pulling the head off of Lily's skunk to reveal a ballpoint pen tip. "You vrite with."

"Thanks!" Lily said. She wasn't sure she was going to be able to write with the thing, but right now, knowing Kresha was behind her *and* Suzy was keeping her from bursting into tears.

"Kresha," Zooey said, "come over here. I have to talk to you about something." She moved a few paces even farther from the bench and beckoned to Kresha impatiently with her hand.

"Vhy we can't talk here?" Kresha said.

"Just come on!" Zooey said.

Kresha frowned as she followed Zooey several yards from where Lily sat feeling like a large swollen toe. She looked uncertainly at Suzy, who was intent on reorganizing her backpack to make room for Kresha's present.

Does she know Zooey asked me to drop out of the contest? Lily thought. *I bet if she did she'd be so mad at Zooey.*

Lily grunted. *I'm so mad at Zooey!*

It was all Lily could think about that morning—until third period when she walked in Mrs. Reinhold's door and Reni grabbed her by the arm.

"Look!" she said. "It's the list!"

It took Lily a moment to get focused on the piece of paper that had been tacked to the small bulletin board just inside the door. Only when Reni stabbed her finger at the name Benjamin Weeks did Lily realize she was looking at the list of all the seventh-grade contestants in the speech contest.

"Why were you just pointing to Benjamin's name?" said a voice behind them.

Reni rolled her eyes at Lily before she turned to Ashley.

"Lily's gonna beat him," Reni said.

"Oh, nuh-uh," Ashley said. "You'll never beat him. He's way cuter to look at — for one thing."

"It's not a beauty contest," Reni said.

"Gee — thanks!" Lily said.

"Besides that," Ashley went on, "he's a way better speaker."

"What's his speech about?" Reni said.

"I don't *know*!" Ashley said, as if Reni had just asked her the average temperature in Katmandu. As she flounced off to her desk, Reni shook her head and muttered something about Ashley being a complete airhead. Lily was busy studying the list.

"There's fourteen people on here," she said.

"So?"

"So — that's a lot of people to beat."

Reni gave her a nudge. "Then you work harder and practice more than any of them. You can *so* do it."

Lily gave Benjamin's name one more long look, and then she nodded and said, "I especially have to beat *him*."

Lily thought about it the whole period as she was looking up the week's vocabulary words in the total silence of Mrs. Reinhold's classroom. It wasn't just Benjamin she wanted to stomp into the ground with her speech. It was his whole crowd — people like Chelsea and Ashley and Bernadette. They took every chance they could dream up to put Lily and the rest of the Girlz down — so why not put them in their place?

I'm not the one who put me in this contest, Lily thought, about the time she was scanning the dictionary page for the word "oxymoron." *But as long as I'm in it, I might as well do my best to win.*

She scribbled down the definition for oxymoron: a figure of speech in which opposite or contradictory ideas or terms are combined, as in "sweet sorrow." Then she got up to put the dictionary on the shelf. Suzy got there three steps behind her.

"Some of those words were stupid," Lily whispered to her. "Who's ever gonna use 'oxymoron' in a sentence?"

Suzy shrugged, stuck her dictionary in with the others, and went back to her seat without saying a word. Lily was still staring at her when Ashley came up and poked Lily in the side with her dictionary.

"Get out of the way," she whispered, and then added in a hoarse voice, "Loser."

But that didn't sting as much as the fact that Suzy didn't wait for Reni and Lily after class or that she and Zooey said they had something else to do during lunch and didn't join them and Kresha at their table in the cafeteria. Lily tried not to think about it. She focused instead on doing what Reni said—working harder than anybody else on her speech.

That night when she'd finished writing all her vocabulary words in sentences—even "oxymoron"— Lily went downstairs to see if anybody was giving a speech on TV. It might help to watch a professional.

Mom was the only one in the family room, and she only vaguely looked up from the papers she was grading when Lily picked up the remote and began to flip through the stations.

"Homework all done?" Mom said.

"Uh-huh—Mom, what's that one cable channel where all they do is talk all day?"

"That's all anybody does on TV, Lil," Mom said.

"No—I mean politicians and stuff."

"Are you talking about C-SPAN?"

"What number is it?"

"Twenty-five, I think."

Lily clicked to it. Some guy was sitting at a microphone, droning on with a deadpan expression on his face. "That's it," Lily said.

"Why in the world do you want to watch this?"

"To get pointers for the speech contest."

Mom grunted. "The only pointers you're going to get from this is how to put your audience to sleep. Why don't you ask your father to help you?"

"Dad?" Lily answered. She considered the idea of her dreamy-eyed, absent-minded father showing her how to be a dynamite speaker—and *she* grunted.

"What?" Mom said. "Your father gives lectures for a living. He's in Philly giving a talk right now."

"Yeah, but that's different," Lily said. "Those are college kids. They *have* to listen to him."

"Those kids get on waiting lists to get into his classes, and I *don't* think it's because they're in love with medieval literature." Mom's mouth twitched. "*He* is, but then, that's him."

Lily thought about it as she switched off Mr. Boring. "I guess I could ask him," she said.

"I'd do it if I were you," Mom said. "And if you want, I might be able to help you some."

Lily tried not to look doubtful. Mom was a phys ed teacher at the high school. Pep talks to the volleyball team in the locker room weren't exactly what Lily had in mind.

"I'm not talking about helping you with your speech," Mom said. "I'm talking about helping you with whatever's on your mind besides that."

Lily looked up quickly. Mom had abandoned the papers and was studying Lily's face. "What's up?" she said.

"Nothing, really," Lily said—and then blurted out the whole thing about Zooey and Suzy.

"Zooey asked you to drop out of the contest?" Mom said when she was finished.

21

"Yeah."

Mom shook her head, ponytail swaying. "Kids these days don't seem to know beans about friendly competition."

"*Friendly* competition?" Lily said. A light went on in her head. "Isn't that what you call an oxymoron?"

"Your generation thinks it is. Whatever happened to competing for the fun of it—enjoying a rivalry—letting the best man win and then going out and celebrating together when it's over?"

"People *do* that?"

"Yes—and I suggest you try to do that with Suzy. I think it would be good for her *and* Zooey."

Lily pondered that for a minute, twirling a red curl around her finger. "How would I do it, though?" she said finally.

"You could invite Suzy over and have Dad coach both of you. If you were working on it together, you'd be invested in each other's doing your best. Then it wouldn't be all about winning."

But it is all about winning, Lily almost said. *At least it's about beating Benjamin.* But she didn't say it. Mom might suggest that she invite him over for coaching too, and that was out of the question.

"I'm gonna go call Suzy," Lily said instead. "When do you think Dad could work with us?"

"I'll ask him when he gets home, which is going to be late. Why don't you just see if she wants to do it?"

"She will," Lily said as she headed toward the kitchen for the phone. After all, Suzy was probably hating this unfriendly competition as much as she was. *In fact,* she decided as she was dialing Suzy's number, *I'm gonna call Zooey next and invite her to come too. When she sees that this isn't about me and Suzy beating each other—*

"Hello?" Suzy said.

"Hi!" Lily said.

There was a funny silence on the other end of the line. Suzy was the quietest one of the Girlz, but when it was just Lily and her, it wasn't usually this hard to carry on a conversation. So far, this was like talking to Lily's dog, Otto. The silence was so awkward that Lily quickly spilled her coaching plan into the receiver.

When Suzy still didn't respond, Lily's stomach started to churn.

"So—do you wanna do it?" she said.

"When?" Suzy said.

"We have to check my dad's schedule," Lily said.

"I don't know if I can." There was another long, stiff pause from Suzy. "I'm pretty busy—"

"But you're gonna practice some time, aren't you?" Lily said.

"Zooey says I don't need to practice that much."

"How does she know? She hasn't even heard your speech."

"Well—" Lily could hear Suzy changing the phone to her other ear. "Zooey says Mrs. Reinhold wouldn't have picked me if I wasn't good."

"She picked me too, but I'm gonna practice!" Lily said.

"You are?" Suzy said. "I mean—like—a lot?"

"Longer and harder than anybody else," Lily said. "That's what Reni says to do—and she oughta know more than Zooey. What did Zooey ever win in her life?"

There was one more wordless moment. Then Suzy said in a clipped voice, "I gotta go."

"Wait!" Lily said. "Do you wanna work with me and my dad or not?"

For the first time, Suzy didn't hesitate. "No thanks," she said. "Bye."

Seconds after she heard the click of Suzy hanging up, Lily was still holding the receiver. In fact, she was still clinging to it when Art came into the kitchen with several dirty dishes.

"Mom says no more snacks 'til she gets all her dishes back," he said. He gave Lily a second look as he headed for the sink. "What's up with you?" he said. "You look like somebody just punched you out."

"Somebody just did," Lily said.

Chapter 3

"Zooey's turning Suzy against me because of this speech contest thing," Lily told Otto that night as she pulled on a pajama T-shirt and boxers and climbed into bed. "And it's stupid because there's no way she's gonna win anyway."

She stopped and looked at her dog, who turned over onto his back and observed his front paws. Yeah, it was a lot like talking to Suzy.

Lily sighed and opened her talking-to-God journal.

God—I have to do the best in this contest, she wrote, *because I can't just let Benjamin win. Kids like him don't deserve it. And besides—I think I've found my thing. I'm good at this speech-giving stuff—only, please don't let Zooey ruin it. Please make her see that it's wrong to turn this into an unfriendly competition. Please.*

Lily turned off her light and snuggled down under the covers. Otto burrowed under them with her and started his nightly paw cleaning. With all the licking-between-the-toes racket and disturbing thoughts circling in her head, it was a while before she could get to sleep.

I want to win, the thought circle began. *Because I wanna be the best. And I wanna beat Benjamin because those kids always think they're all that. Only I don't wanna hurt Suzy's feelings. She's gonna freak out when she sees all the people in the audience. I could help her, only she won't let me 'cause Zooey's turning her against me. The only way I could stop that is if I dropped out. But I wanna win—because I wanna be the best.*

The circle kept on long after Otto had cleaned both feet and fallen asleep.

I gotta stop this whole thing, she thought as she flopped over for about the fiftieth time. *I'm gonna talk to the Girlz first thing in the morning.*

It was the first thought on Lily's mind when Otto licked her face at 6:00 am—right after the thought that he was using the same tongue he'd used to bathe his feet. She shoved him off the bed just as the door opened and Mom poked her head in.

"I know what I'm gonna do about the Suzy thing," Lily said, shoving aside Otto's attempt to jump back up on the bed.

Mom's mouth twitched. "Good morning to you too, Lil," she said.

"Yeah, I'm just gonna come right out and talk about it before first period when we're all at the bench."

"Sounds like a plan," Mom said. "Only I was going to suggest that if you really want to get ahead with your speech, you ought to go to Mrs. Reinhold before school and ask her to help you."

"Dad can't do it?" Lily said.

"Try and stop him," Mom said. Her almost-smile appeared again. "I gave him a heads-up when he got home last night. He's chomping at the bit to get with you. But you said you wanted to win this thing big time, so it can't hurt to hit up Mrs. Reinhold too."

Lily nodded. She was still blinking the sleep out of her eyes, but her mind was already racing.

"I could be ready in time to ride with you so I could get there way early," she said, once more shoving Otto and his tongue out of the way.

"At least you won't have to bother washing your face," Mom said.

Lily didn't even take the time to say, "Gross me out and make me icky." She hauled out of bed. She was on a mission.

The halls were still almost completely empty when Mom dropped Lily off, and Lily hoped she hadn't beaten Mrs. Reinhold there.

But it'll be okay to be waiting outside her door when she does get here, Lily thought. It never hurt to impress Mrs. Reinhold.

The door was propped open when Lily rounded the corner. She slowed down to peek into the glass to make sure there was no stray hair hanging in her eyes and that her face hadn't gone all blotchy the way it did when she got worked up. She needed to make sure Mrs. Reinhold knew she was cool and confident about this.

But as Lily took one last glimpse in the glass in the door, satisfied that she looked as together as any TV anchorwoman, she heard a voice inside the room.

It was Suzy talking.

"So if it isn't too much trouble," she was saying, "I wondered if you could maybe give me some extra help."

"I think that's an excellent idea, Suzanne," Mrs. Reinhold said. "Your speech is very good, and frankly you surprised me with your delivery—but it certainly can't hurt to give it some polish."

"I really want to practice a lot," Suzy said.

"I'm impressed," Mrs. Reinhold said. "That kind of thinking will make you a winner. Now let me look at my schedule—"

Lily didn't wait for Mrs. Reinhold to start penciling Suzy in. She backed silently away from the door, and as soon as she could do it without being heard by either of them, she stormed toward the stairs, face burning in one big blotch.

Oh, please! she fumed as she took the steps down. *First she tells me Zooey says she doesn't need to practice, and then the minute I say I'm going to get help and practice a lot, she goes straight to Mrs. Reinhold! She is so—hateful!*

Lily stopped on the bottom step—hand on the rail. Had she just called Suzy "hateful"? Quiet little Suzy Wheeler, her best friend next to Reni?

Well, she is! Lily thought, clutching the stair rail even harder. *She was in there acting all sweet with Mrs. Reinhold, trying to impress her.*

And what was worse, it was working. Hadn't Mrs. Reinhold come right out and said she was impressed that Suzy had come to her for help?

Huh, Lily thought. *Mrs. Reinhold doesn't know Suzy like we do. She doesn't know Suzy's gonna take one look at all those people in the audience and freeze up like an ice cube.* Lily gave her head a toss. *And I hope she does. See if I try to help her any more—ever again.*

"What are you doing, Robbins, having a fight with yourself?"

Lily jerked around. Shad Shifferdecker was on his way up the steps, his usual smirk playing around his lips. Although Lily and Shad weren't rivals the way they'd been in sixth grade, whenever she saw him, it always took Lily a few seconds to remember that.

"No," she said. "I'm just ticked off at somebody." She started to take the last step down.

"You want me to take care of 'em for you?" Shad said.

Lily stopped. "What?" she said.

"You want me to get 'em for you?"

"Who?"

"Whoever you're mad at." Shad's smirk worked its way slowly into an evil grin. "I'm pretty good at it," he said.

For an instant, Lily had an image of Suzy opening her locker to the explosion of a Shad-placed stink bomb. But if she got caught being in cahoots with Shad, she wouldn't just get booted out of the speech contest, she'd get tossed out of school—not to mention her house!

She shook her head.

"That's okay," she said. "I'll take care of it."

"Whatever," Shad said. "If you change your mind, look me up."

"Yeah," Lily said absently. And then she went to look Reni up.

But Reni was rehearsing in the orchestra room, and Lily didn't get to talk to her about Suzy until right before third period. By then she'd been thinking about it so much that she was starting to break out in hives.

"It's out of control!" Lily said when she'd told Reni about this latest development.

"Nah—you're still gonna win," Reni said.

"But that's not the point! Suzy and Zooey are—"

"Forget them," Reni said. "You gotta focus on being the best. Trust me—I know what I'm talking about."

Lily took a deep breath. "I'm doing that. My dad's gonna coach me—he'd coach Suzy too, only she's being all hateful about it."

"How are you gonna win if you're helping the competition?" Reni said. "Concentrate on what you gotta do."

"Yeah, huh?"

"Yeah." Reni gave her a poke in the ribs. "Come on, Lil—you're the one who always makes everything into a career. Do it like you did modeling and that doctor thing and being all Martha Stewart about your party and—"

"Okay, I get it," Lily said. "I gotta make a list of stuff to do." The wheels started spinning in her head. "I wonder if Mrs. Reinhold will let me go to the library this period. I bet they have speeches on videotape."

Reni grinned. "That's the Lily I know."

"I'm sorry," Ashley said as she swept past them and into Mrs. Reinhold's room.

But it didn't faze Lily. She had plans to make.

She zipped through the drills on subject-verb agreement and then started on her list:

1. Get speeches on video — Martin Luther King, Jr. and — some other people — ask librarian
2. Watch people make speeches on TV
3. Work with Dad every night — maybe mornings too — get up at 5:00 am
4. Videotape myself giving my speech and study it

She felt a lot better when she'd finished the list, and she wrote Reni a Girlz-Gram to tell her. In fact, she felt so much better, she decided to write one to Suzy too — something like, *May the best girl win*, or something —

But the bell rang, and she had to figure out how she was going to get to the library after school and still make it to Girlz Only. The best thing to do, she thought, was to tell Zooey she'd be late. And she would do it with a smile. Just because Zooey and Suzy were being hateful didn't mean she had to be.

But when she finally caught up with Zooey in the lunch line, she barely got out, "Zooey, I'm gonna be a little late this afternoon—" when Zooey cut her off.

"Then you probably shouldn't even bother," she said, inspecting the selection of sandwiches on the counter, "because we're leaving right from my house at 3:15."

"Who?" Lily said.

"All of us." Zooey picked up a turkey on wheat and examined it through its plastic wrap. "All the Girlz."

"Leaving for where?"

"To go shopping — for an outfit for Suzy to do her speech in. Her mom doesn't have time to take her, so my mom said she would — so it's our Girlz Only thing for today."

"How come nobody told me?" Lily said.

Zooey put the sandwich on her tray and scooted it down the rail. She had yet to look Lily in the eye. "I'm telling you now," she said. "And besides, you just said you can't make it."

29

Then she turned her full attention to the fruit selection. Lily left the line. She'd just lost her appetite.

Reni was in the orchestra room during lunch that day, and Lily managed to get to her before she got her violin out of the case.

"Reni!" she said when she'd barely entered the room. "Why didn't you tell me everybody's going shopping for Suzy's outfit today after school?"

"Who's everybody?" Reni said.

"All the Girlz."

Reni set down her case and put her hands on her hips. "I don't even know what you're talking about, girl."

Lily filled her in. By the time she was finished, Reni's neck was stretched up like E.T.'s, and her eyes were blazing.

"That girl needs to get a clue!" Reni said. "Who does she think she is makin' plans for everybody without even asking?"

"That's what I—"

"And who died and left her in charge of who wants who to win this contest?"

"I don't know—I just—"

"If Zooey thinks I'm gonna go help get Miss Suzy Snot-Ball all fixed up to impress everybody, she can just think again. But I am goin' to the library with you after school, and then I am going with you to the video store, and then you and I are gonna practice that speech until you can do it backward and upside down!" Her dark eyes narrowed down to slits. "We are gonna show those two," she said.

To Lily it was as if a line had just been drawn in the dirt and Zooey and Suzy were on the other side of it. But at least Reni was taking her place on Lily's side.

"Well?" Reni said.

"Yeah," Lily said. "Okay."

Chapter 4

For the next several days, the contest was all Lily could think about.

The movie store didn't have any videos of speeches — in fact, the kid behind the counter looked at her and Reni like they were asking for movies in Russian. But they did check out several from the school library, and Lily watched them until she almost had "I Have a Dream" and President Kennedy's inaugural speech memorized.

Reni helped her talk Art into videotaping her speech before Dad started helping her so she would have a "before" speech to see how much she improved. Art did it only when she promised to give him all her phone time for the rest of the week. Even then, he would only do three takes of her speech before he told her she really ought to switch to decaf.

Dad coached her every evening for at least an hour, though he drew the line at doing sessions at 5:00 am.

"Nobody can even make sense at that hour, Lilliputian," he told her.

"But if I want to win, I have to," she said.

"I wasn't talking about you," he said, blue eyes twinkling. "I was talking about me."

Mom also put the kibosh on Lily practicing her speech at the dinner table, but she did promise Lily a new outfit for the competition, and they went shopping Thursday night.

It feels good to have all these people on my side, Lily wrote in her journal when she and Mom got home. *Thanks for blessing me, God.*

The only thing that didn't feel good was how strained things were with the Girlz. Zooey and Suzy were acting like they had their own club now, and Kresha kept running back and forth between them and Lily and Reni before school and during lunch and after school, asking, "Vhy ve not friends? Vhy ve fight?"

"We're not fighting, Kresha," Reni told her before school Friday when Kresha found her and Lily hanging out in front of the orchestra room instead of at the bench. "They're the ones who started it."

Kresha's eyes scrunched together. "Vhat they start?"

"The fight," Reni said.

"Oh," Kresha said. Her eyes practically met over her nose.

It was confusing to Lily too, but she kept trying to focus on practicing. She was all ready to make her presentation to Dad that evening, but he had to take Joe to hockey practice. "Hey, why don't you come along?" he asked.

"Okay," Lily said, grabbing her coat and her note cards. "I can rehearse for you in the car."

"Aw, man, does she have to?" Joe wailed. "I'm hearing that speech in my sleep!"

"You want me to win, don't you?" Lily said.

Joe pulled his hockey mask down over his face.

"I think your brother's been very patient with all this," Dad said, putting his arm around Joe's shoulder and steering him toward the garage. "But I wouldn't push it." He lowered his voice to a whisper. "He does have a hockey stick in his hand."

So what am I supposed to do through this whole hockey practice? Lily thought as she trailed behind them out to the van. *I can't be wasting valuable rehearsal time!*

"Maybe I should stay here, Dad," she said.

Dad just opened the van door and pointed. Lily climbed in.

It had been a long time since Lily had been to any of Joe's games or practices. Ever since she'd started middle school, she'd been too busy, and besides, Joe was in so many sports, who could keep up with it all?

Watching Joe take the ice, his body already taut with the anticipation of a slap shot, it occurred to her that Joe wanted to win at his thing as much as she did at hers. Right now, even though his face was covered with his mask, she could tell by the way he went after the sliding puck that he was looking like the Terminator underneath it. Lily nudged her father.

"Do you think being competitive runs in our family?" she said.

Dad adjusted his glasses and tilted his head. It was one of the things she loved about him. He almost always took her seriously.

"I think we all go after what we want," he said finally. "But I'm not sure whether that's nature or nurture."

"Huh?" Lily said.

"I don't know whether you were all born that way or you've learned from us to always do your best."

Lily nodded toward Joe, who was currently chasing down the puck like it had just bitten him and he was going to beat it with the stick. "He's not just doing his best," she said. "He looks like he wants to deck somebody."

Dad chuckled. "He gets that from your mother, then. I never go after the prize quite that hard."

"I must take after her too, then," Lily said. "'Cause I really want to win this speech contest. I mean, really, really."

"Why is that?" Dad said. He took off his glasses, surveyed her closely, and then put them back on.

"Why?" Lily said. "Um—because like you said, you and Mom always taught us to be the best. Plus, I'm good at it. I don't mean to be conceited or anything, but Mrs. Reinhold did pick me, and you even told me I'm doing good."

"Go on."

"And I really want to show Benjamin and the popular kids that they don't get to be on top at everything—not in the things that count."

"I see," Dad said.

Lily wasn't sure exactly what it was Dad saw. It didn't appear to be good, not the way he was now chewing on the earpiece of his glasses.

"So—have you talked to God about all this?" he asked.

"Oh, yeah!" Lily said. She felt relieved. So that was what he was worried about. "I pray about it every night, Dad. I keep asking God to help me do my best and help me win. And I keep asking him not to let this mess up my friendships. He's being a little slow on that one, but I know about things having to happen in God's time and all that."

"I see," he said again. And again he didn't look as if he exactly liked what he was seeing.

"You know, Lilliputian—" he said.

But before he could finish his sentence, the whistle down on the court blew long and loud—longer and louder than it had all practice. Suddenly, it was as if everyone on the ice was streaming over to one corner. The coach was shouting above them all as he skated toward the group.

"What's going on down there?" Dad said. He stood up and fumbled to put his glasses on. Something about the way everybody was suddenly quiet made Lily feel stiff. She stood up too, in time to see one of the assistant coaches break out of the knot of boys and parents and search the bleachers. When he waved at Dad, Lily felt herself stop breathing.

"Joe's hurt," Dad said — and he took the bleachers down two benches at a time.

Lily almost didn't follow him. She didn't want to see her little brother crumpled up on the ice with a hockey puck up his nose.

But she did take off after Dad, heart pounding, and it wasn't quite as bad as her imagination had painted it by the time they got down to Joe. Still, it was bad enough. He was lying on his back, eyes closed, face as pale as the ice, with one leg bent in an awkward position. Joe Robbins never looked awkward.

"I think we should call 9-1-1," the coach said to Dad.

Dad gave a grim nod. He was already on his knees beside Joe, and his face was even grayer than Joe's.

"I'll call Mom," Lily said, and with shaking fingers, she took the cell phone from Dad.

After that, things happened in that dreamlike, almost-slow-motion way that they do in an emergency. The paramedics came — Joe woke up, his big brown eyes wide with fear — and Dad and Lily followed the ambulance to Rancocas Hospital in the van at breakneck speed. Mom met them all in the parking lot. Her face looked so pinched it was as if she had pulled her ponytail too tight. Lily knew it was fear.

Mom and Dad left Lily in the waiting room while they went with Joe, who was now moaning mournfully as guys in green outfits pushed him behind some curtains.

"That's a good sign," the nurse told Lily, and then he, too, left her alone on a blue plastic chair to wonder how Joe bleating like a calf could possibly be a good sign.

Lily sagged in the chair and closed her eyes. *Please, God, please,* she prayed. *Let him be okay. He's a pain, but he's my brother. Please let him be okay.*

Art arrived in his pep band uniform, and Dad came out of the examining room at the same time — about the time Lily was praying and wringing her hands so hard they were turning red.

"What's up?" Art said. Lily had never seen him so pale. He looked twelve years old again.

"Good news," Dad said. He adjusted his glasses—then adjusted them again.

"Is he gonna be okay?" Lily said. "Do they have to do an operation? He's gonna hate that. He hates not being awake and knowing everything that's going on."

Art put his arm around Lily's neck and covered her mouth with his hand. "Go ahead, Dad," he said.

As Lily shook Art's hand away, Dad put one of his on each of them, squeezing their shoulders.

"He's going to be fine," he said. "He's suffered a concussion, but they're certain there's been no brain damage."

"Not like you could tell," Art said. He was already grinning.

"No internal injuries," Dad went on, "but he does have a pretty serious leg fracture that has to be taken care of." He looked at Lily. "He will have to have surgery. They're prepping him for that right now."

"Can we see him before he goes under the knife?" Art said.

Dad's eyebrows rose over the rims of his glasses. "Only if you don't use terminology like that. He's putting up a pretty good front, but he's scared. He's upset because this is going to take him out for the rest of the hockey season and probably spring soccer."

"Who cares?" Lily said. "At least he's alive!"

"You're so dramatic," Art said.

"You didn't see him lying there on the ice," Lily said. "I thought he was gonna die. He was so white."

"He's going to be fine," Dad said. "But he needs to see smiles on both of you, or you don't go in."

Dad rarely got the I-mean-business look on his face, so when he did, the Robbins kids shaped up. Lily put on a dazzling smile, and Art immediately went into fully casual mode, hands stuffed easily into his pockets and eyes at half-mast.

It was hard, at least for Lily, to keep up the cheerful thing when Dad ushered them into a curtained-off cubicle. Mom was stroking one of Joe's arms, while a taped-down needle going into a vein occupied the other. He was wearing a blue gown that was so big it would have fit Art and Lily together and a matching hat that looked like the one Mom wore in the shower when she didn't want to get her hair wet.

"Nice cap, dude," Art said.

"Shut up," Joe said.

He tried to grin, but Lily could see that his lips were trembling. She was having a hard time keeping her own lips under control.

"So you spazzed out, huh?" Art said.

"I didn't spaz out," Joe said. "It was Brandon Warren. He comes at me from the left, and boom." He tried to demonstrate with the taped-up arm, setting the plastic bag of liquid that was running into him swinging.

"Slow down, pal," Mom said. "You can give us all the brutal details later. You're going to have plenty of time."

"Yeah, did you guys hear?" Joe said. His eyes drooped. "I'm out for the rest of the season."

"That's a bummer," Art said.

Lily nodded and tried to look sympathetic, but she still didn't get it. Who could think about ever picking up a hockey stick again when he was about to be put to sleep, cut open, and stitched up?

She hoped Joe didn't see her shudder, and she was relieved when the nurse came in and said they were taking Joe up to the operating room.

"Why don't you two go home?" Mom said as they wheeled him out. "We'll call you as soon as he's done."

"You sure you don't want us to stay?" Art said. "You and Dad gonna be okay?"

To Lily's amazement, always calm Mom threw her arms around Art's neck and squeezed him hard. Her voice sounded thick, as she said, "No—we'll be fine. You guys go on." Her eyes looked red and watery as she turned to hug Lily.

"You're not okay, Mom," Art said. "Look at you—you're a mess."

"I'm just sad for Joe," Mom said. "He's going to be fine, I know that. But he's so upset about the season. Poor little guy."

She practically shoved them toward the door at that point, and Lily and Art went out to the parking lot.

"Dude, look at the way I parked," Art said when they got to the car. He gave a sheepish grin. "I was having visions of Joe with tubes coming out of his nose and stuff. I'm surprised I didn't get a ticket driving over here. I was goin' down Route 130 at about 90 miles an hour."

"How did you find out, anyway?" Lily said as they buckled up and took off for home.

"I went back to the house after the game to get my money 'cause we were all going out for pizza. It looked like Mom had left in a hurry, which weirded me out." He gave Lily a sideways glance. "She doesn't usually leave her bathrobe in the middle of the kitchen floor."

"She said she'd just gotten out of the shower when I called," Lily said.

"Anyway, I knew something was up, so I listened to the messages on the answering machine. I had to get through one for you before I finally got Mom saying Joe was at the hospital and all that." Art shook his head as he turned the defroster up. "Man, I always thought I was cool in a crisis, but I about lost it on the way over there. If anything really bad ever happened to that little punk, I'd probably totally freak."

They were both quiet for a few blocks. It gave Lily too much space to think about Joe right now lying on an operating table.

"So—" she said just to break the silence. "Who was my message from?"

"I don't know—it was weird."

"What kind of weird?"

"A prank. Somebody messing around." Art glanced at her as he turned the corner onto their street. "What did you do to tick somebody off?"

"Nothing," Lily said.

"You must of done something. People don't say stuff like 'You are such a loser' unless you ticked them off."

"Somebody did *not* say that on our answering machine!" Lily said.

"Listen for yourself," Art said.

When they got to the house, Lily did listen—after first picking up Mom's bathrobe, slippers, and towel. Art had been right. There was a weird message on their machine, saying in a muffled voice, "This is for Lily. You're a loser, and you need to drop out of the speech contest. Like—today."

"So who is it?" Art said.

"I don't recognize the voice," Lily said. She listened to it again, but then she had to stop. Whoever it was, the person obviously hated her guts. The voice had a nasty edge to it that made her feel sick to her stomach.

"I think I'm gonna throw up," Lily said.

"Yeah, it's been a rough night," Art said. "Do we have any of those frozen pizzas?"

Lily passed on the pizza and sat poking at the ice in a glass of ginger ale while Art flipped channels and they waited for Mom to call. Lily went back and forth like a seesaw. One minute she was worrying about Joe, and the next she was wondering who hated her so much that they'd leave her such a hateful message.

Well, du-uh, she thought finally. *It was so Ashley. She already told me to my face I was a loser.*

That was kind of a no-brainer, in fact. Ashley and her friends had threatened Lily in the past when it looked like she might come out ahead of somebody in their group.

I don't really need to worry about them, she told herself. *I've got the Girlz to help protect me. They always do.*

Or at least, they always had before. Now, maybe the only one she could count on was Reni. She felt a lump in her throat. It was too much for one night.

The phone rang just then, and Art and Lily jumped for it. Having more practice with phone technique, Art got to it first. He started to smile right after he said hello, and he held out the receiver so Lily could hear.

"The surgery went well," Mom said. "Joe's in recovery, and if everything continues to go okay, he'll be able to come home tomorrow afternoon."

"That's awesome," Art told her. "How you holdin' up?"

"Me?" Mom said. "I'm fine. Your father has had five cups of coffee, though. I need to go peel him off the wall."

Lily could almost see Mom's mouth twitching. It made her want to cry with relief.

"Go on to bed," she heard Mom tell Art. "Let's try to get back to normal. The crisis is over."

Lily was happy to go curl up with Otto. She was too tired to write in her God journal, but she did pray before she drifted off.

God—you showed us it's true—if we're believing and we're praying, you'll give us what we want. Now that the crisis is over—and even Mom said so—please make people stop hating me. They just don't want me to win.

"But I'm gonna win anyway, Otto," she whispered sleepily. "I'm gonna work harder and practice more. And I've got God on my side."

Chapter 5

There was a lot to do on Saturday to get the family room ready for Joe to hang out and sleep in, since getting up and down the steps to his own room was going to be hard for a while.

"Aw, man," Art said as he and Dad hauled Joe's bed downstairs. "He's gonna think he owns the remote."

"He *is* going to be in proximity to the television the majority of the time, isn't he?" Dad said. "We're going to have to set some parameters."

Art glanced over his shoulder at Lily. "How come I can't understand a thing he says half the time?" he said.

Lily understood enough to be relieved. There was a documentary on the Gettysburg Address that night on the History Channel that she had planned to watch. She was about to ask for dibs on that hour when the phone rang. She started to go for it and then stopped. What if it was Ashley or somebody pranking her again? It was one thing to hear it on tape but something else to get an earful of that in person.

"Lilliputian, could you get that?" Dad said. The veins in his neck were bulging under the weight of the mattress as he and Art dragged it into the family room.

"Could you get it, Art?" Lily said.

"Uh—how about no? My third arm isn't working."

The phone rang again, and Lily picked it up as if it were going to burn her fingers. "Hello?" she whispered into the receiver.

"Lee-lee?" said the voice on the other end.

Lily let out a huge breath. It was Kresha. Lily hardly heard her first few sentences, because her heart was beating so loudly in her ears. She tuned in just in time to hear Kresha say, "So I can go to church—you church—tomorrow, Lee-lee?"

"Huh?" Lily said. "You want to go to my church?"

"Ya. Vit you."

Lily tried not to stutter as she answered. Although Kresha always seemed to like to join in when the Girlz joined hands to pray, she'd never shown an interest in going to church. But right now, she sounded pretty excited.

"So—I can come?" Kresha said.

"Well, sure," Lily said. "And you want to go with me? I mean—not Suzy?"

Lily wasn't sure why she'd asked that—it had just popped out. But now that she'd said it, she held her breath waiting for Kresha's answer.

"Ya," Kresha said, stretching the word into several syllables. "It is o-kay?"

"Absolutely," Lily said. "Maybe you could spend the night tonight so we can just go together in the morning. Let me ask my mom when she gets home." She then launched into the tale of Joe's accident. Before she knew it, she and Kresha were planning ways to entertain Joe through the evening.

As it turned out, Joe was on pain medication when he got home, and he slept most of the evening. Kresha and Lily were deep into the documentary on Lincoln's Gettysburg Address—at least Lily was; Kresha spent most of the time squinting, puzzled, at the TV—when the phone rang.

Lily pretended not to hear it. Art was out for the evening. Joe was zonked in the bed. Mom and Dad were upstairs, probably zonked out themselves. By the time Lily sighed and moved slowly toward it, the answering machine picked it up. Lily waited next to it.

When the machine beeped, a voice that sounded like it was coming out of a mouth full of cotton balls said, "Lily Robbins, get a clue. You're a loser—you can't win—you better drop out. Don't say you weren't warned."

Lily wanted to rip the plug to the answering machine out of the wall, but she could feel Kresha at her elbow, so she tried to shrug. It came off more like a twitch in her shoulders.

"It's Ashley and her friends again," Lily said, trying hard to sound as if it didn't bother her in the least. "They're just trying to scare me."

"Ve can hear again?" Kresha said.

"How about no!" Lily said. "It was hard enough the first time!"

But Kresha reached for the play button, and Lily had to pull Kresha's hand back to stop her from pushing it.

"I'm not gonna let them get to me, Kresha," Lily said. "I'm gonna work harder and practice more than Benjamin—or anybody—so they can call me all they want."

Still, Kresha looked longingly at the answering machine. Lily tugged on the sleeve of the big T-shirt Kresha had put on for pajamas.

"Come on," Lily said. "We'll make some popcorn."

Kresha usually went nuts over popcorn. She obviously hadn't had much of it in Croatia. But that night, she barely nibbled on a few pieces, and she was quiet as Lily rambled on about every subject she could think of. Lily wasn't sure that Kresha heard half of what Lily said. Some of the time she even forgot to say, "Uh-huh."

Oh, no, Lily thought when Kresha rolled over on her half of Lily's bed and went to sleep. *I hope she's not mad at me. I hope she's not gonna go over to Suzy and Zooey's side.* The thought reminded her of that imaginary line Reni had drawn and how sick it made her feel.

Lily fell into a fitful sleep and woke up with a start a short time later. There was a noise in the room, and it took her a confused moment to realize it was Otto, digging into the leftover popcorn.

"No way," Lily said as she scrambled out of bed and snatched the bowl away from him. "You'll be puking all over my rug."

Holding the bowl over her head, Lily tiptoed out of the room and down the stairs to put it back in the kitchen. She was dumping the leftovers in the trashcan when she heard another noise, this time from the direction of the family room.

Joe! she thought.

Lily hurried through the dining room and into the family room. Mom had left a night-light on for him, and in its glow, Lily could see Joe sitting up on one elbow.

"Are you okay?" Lily whispered.

He didn't answer, at least not in words. But something that sounded like a sob erupted from the bed.

"Does it hurt bad?" Lily said. "You want me to get Mom?"

"No," Joe said. His voice choked, and he sobbed again — and then again — and then again. Lily went to him and sat on the edge of the bed. She couldn't see his face, because he was hiding it behind his hands.

"It really hurts, huh?" Lily said. "Is it time for a pill or something?" Joe shook his head.

"Then how come you're crying?" Lily said. "You never cry."

"I'm gonna miss everything," he said. He sniffed and grabbed for the sheet, which he used to wipe his nose.

Gross me out and make me icky, Lily thought. But she felt too sorry for Joe to say it. She was sure she hadn't seen him cry since —

Lily stopped in the middle of her thought and switched to another one: she hadn't seen Joe cry since his Little League team had lost the county championship two years before.

So that's it, Lily told herself. *Winning is huge for him. He hates being out of hockey because he wants to win—just like I do!*

Lily pulled a Kleenex out of the box for Joe and handed it to him.

"I know your pain," Lily said. "I'd hate it if I had to miss out like that."

Joe watched her with wet eyes as he blew his nose.

"You get it?" he said.

Lily nodded. "I *so* get it." She pulled her legs into a hug and considered her knees. "I know this won't make you feel better right away, but do you want me to pray for you? I've pretty much learned that really works. You're gonna get better faster than most people do."

"You think?" Joe said.

"I know," Lily said.

"Huh," Joe said. And then he lay back on his pillows and nodded off. Lily waited until he was breathing deep and hard before she went back up to her room. She fell asleep herself, praying for Joe.

Kresha was still quiet the next morning, even though Lily let her wear her best sweater and made her favorite breakfast—bagels and peanut butter. Lily was convinced Kresha was going to go over to the Suzy/Zooey side, and all the way to church in the van, she ransacked her brain trying to figure out what had turned her.

But the minute she stepped into the Sunday school room and the middle-school youth advisor made a big fuss over Kresha and gave her a nametag, Kresha started coming out of it. By the time they struck up the first praise song on the guitar, Kresha's eyes were sparkling again, and she was leaning happily against Lily as she sang.

But Lily barely noticed—across the room, Suzy had arrived. And right next to her was her guest, Zooey.

Lily grabbed Reni around the neck and whispered in her ear, "What's Zooey doing here? I thought her mom wouldn't let her go to church now."

Reni shrugged and whispered back, "I guess Suzy brought her."

Any other time, that would have had Lily grinning. Ever since they'd formed Girlz Only, Zooey's mom had said it was okay for Zooey to hang out with them and even fixed up her basement for them. But one thing she would not do was let Zooey go to church with them. She said she didn't want Zooey getting too mixed up with religion until she was old enough to decide for herself, or something like that.

Even now, it lifted Lily's spirits a little to see Zooey there, looking around as if she expected somebody to try to baptize her any minute. But as Lily watched her, Zooey seemed to feel Lily's eyes on her, and she looked up. Their gazes met, and Lily smiled.

Zooey didn't.

Instead, she nudged Suzy and nodded toward Lily, Kresha, and Reni. The looks that froze their faces made them look like twins—eyes in identical slits, cheeks pinched, mouths stiff as icicles. It was enough to freeze the smile on Lily's face.

"Well, excuse me for livin'," Reni whispered to Lily. "Are they bein' hateful or what?"

Maybe they're just surprised to see Kresha here, Lily thought.

But she couldn't convince herself, not the way Suzy and Zooey tilted their chins and turned their bodies so they wouldn't have to look at Kresha, Reni, and Lily.

Lily felt a pang all the way down to her toes.

They were all there—all the Girlz were in church. But they weren't together, and to Lily that felt worse than if some of them hadn't been there at all. It formed a lump in her stomach that made her feel sick again. She turned away from them too, so it wouldn't hurt any worse.

It didn't seem to faze Kresha very much. She was so thrilled with the Sunday school class, so jazzed with the singing, so awed by the worship service and the stained glass windows in the church, that it was all she could talk about the next morning on the bench before school. Lily heard only about a third of it. Besides being upset about the Girlz, she was way too nervous about that night's competition. She hadn't even been able to eat breakfast.

"You don't have any reason to be scared," Reni told her before third period that day. "You are *so* ready. I bet you get up in the middle of the night to practice."

She was interrupted by Mrs. Reinhold beckoning to Lily from the doorway.

"I need to speak with you, Lilianna," she said.

Lily, of course, hurried into the room. Suzy was already at Mrs. Reinhold's desk.

"I want to inform you two how things will be handled this evening," Mrs. Reinhold said. "You'll be more confident if there are no surprises."

Lily barely heard her. It was the first time in almost a week that she had been this close to Suzy, and it was making her hands sweat.

Look at me, Suzy! Lily wanted to say to her. *Squeeze my hand or something. We can be nervous together!*

But Suzy neither spoke nor looked nor squeezed. She kept her eyes glued to Mrs. Reinhold, who was talking about judges and points and order of performance.

"The teachers drew names out of the hat for order," Mrs. Reinhold said. "Lilianna, you will be tenth, which is close to the end. Suzanne—" Mrs. Reinhold looked at Suzy over the top of her teeny glasses. "Now don't panic, but you are first."

Lily heard Suzy catch her breath, and when she looked over, Suzy's face was bone white.

Before she thought, Lily said, "It'll be okay."

Suzy started to look at her, but she quickly pointed her chin away.

47

"I know," she said. "You don't have to tell me that."

Lily wanted to climb into Mrs. Reinhold's desk drawer. She knew she was blotchy right down to her knees.

"All right," Mrs. Reinhold said, "I think you're both ready. I'm sure you'll do very well."

"Thank you," Suzy murmured.

Oh, Suzy, Lily thought. *How are you gonna give a speech? You're going to die up there! You can hardly talk right now. I'm so scared, I'm about to puke, so you must be going nuts. I could so help you.*

Suddenly, Lily realized that she was looking at Suzy, begging her with her eyes. But Suzy was missing it. She was staring straight ahead, refusing to give Lily so much as a glance.

"Did you see how she was acting to me when Mrs. Reinhold was talking to us?" Lily said to Reni at lunch that day. She nodded toward Suzy, who was two tables over with Zooey and, at the moment, Kresha. Any minute now, Kresha would probably be joining Reni and Lily for a few minutes before flitting back to the other side.

"Forget them," Reni said. "You have to focus on your speech. Are you gonna practice after school?"

"Yeah," Lily said. "Art's gonna tape me so I can compare with my 'before' tape."

"Yeah, that'll make you feel good, seeing how far you've come," Reni said.

But Lily knew what would really make her feel good would be praying with all the Girlz in Zooey's basement and having them all give her hugs and sending her Girlz-Grams all day to keep her confidence up. She sighed as she looked over at Zooey and Suzy with their heads together over their nachos. That wasn't going to happen.

Art got home from school in time to tape Lily one more time, and she had to pry the remote out of Joe's hand to get him to give up the TV long enough for her to watch it.

It was definitely different from her first tape, where she'd tucked her hair behind her ears every other second and said "uh" about a hundred times. This one was practically perfect, in fact. She looked straight at the camera, barely blinking, and the words came out of her mouth so smoothly she barely recognized her own voice. When she turned it off, Joe said, "Was that really you?"

"Yeah," Lily said, feeling a bit better. If Joe was impressed, that had to mean something.

What meant more was that Mom got one of the ladies from the church to stay with Joe so she, Dad, and Art could all go to Lily's competition. She tried not to think about how much better she would feel if Zooey and Suzy were sitting with her family and Reni. Once she won this and went on to the countywide competition, Suzy would see how silly she'd been and it would be okay. That kept her from excusing herself from the speakers' section to go throw up. She took deep breaths until Mr. Tanini, the principal, got up to the microphone. Then she stopped breathing.

While he was welcoming the parents and saying how proud he was of all the competitors, Lily sneaked a look at the other speakers. Most of the kids were as still as statues, except for twitching hands or feet that wouldn't keep still. Suzy was absolutely stony; she wasn't even blinking. The only person who looked relaxed was Benjamin. In fact, he looked as if he couldn't have cared less whether he was there or not. Lily sat up straighter in her seat. It suddenly occurred to her that none of his crowd had said anything to her about the speeches since the list was posted last week, except for the phone calls. Lily glanced at the audience. Unless they were hiding somewhere, Ashley and Chelsea and the rest of them didn't appear to even be there.

Huh, Lily thought, *so all those prank phone calls were just a big bluff—and I didn't fall for it.*

Her confidence inched up a little, and she concentrated on Mr. Tanini, who was now introducing Suzy.

Man, she's gotta be so scared, Lily thought. *God, please help her get through this, even though she's been so mean to me about it. I just don't want to see her be humiliated up there.*

As the audience broke into polite applause, Suzy stood and went up to the stage. Her head was high, her shoulders were straight, and when she got to the podium, she smiled at the crowd.

"A person without a purpose in life," Suzy said clearly into the microphone, "is like a ship without a rudder."

Lily knew her mouth was falling open as she watched and listened, but she couldn't help it. Suzy was speaking like she gave a speech every night. Her face was shiny, her voice was strong and warm, and her words sounded like polished conversation.

When she finished, the rest of the audience burst into clapping that lasted after Suzy sat down. Lily applauded too, but every clap stung the palms of her hands.

Suzy had given a perfect speech.

Chapter 6

Well—" Mr. Tanini said when the applause for Suzy finally died down. "That certainly sets the standard, doesn't it?"

Lily wasn't sure, but she thought that meant if everybody else wasn't as good as Suzy, they were morons.

I am a moron! Lily thought. *I should've dropped out when Zooey told me to! I'm gonna look like an idiot up there!*

The next speaker was introduced—a girl in Mrs. Reinhold's other class who Lily didn't know. Lily didn't even try to listen to what she was saying. Her thoughts were out-shouting everything else.

I look like a robot next to Suzy.

I'm gonna open my mouth and nothing's even gonna come out.

I gotta practice in my head right now. What's my first line? Oh, my gosh—I can't think of my first line!

I'm gonna throw up.

There was a spattering of applause and a few loud cheers—probably from the speaker's family. Lily watched her retreat to her seat the way Otto scooted under the bed when he'd been caught chewing a shoe. It was obvious that her speech hadn't gone as well as Suzy's.

And neither did the ones that followed. Nobody bombed, and some kids got more applause than others. But by the time they got to Benjamin, who was number nine, Lily felt like she was sunk. Maybe if she pretended to be sick, no one would blame her if she dropped out now. She wouldn't have to do much pretending. As Benjamin walked to the podium like some bad boy approaching the neighborhood basketball court, Lily realized she was sweating so badly her hair was damp at the neck, and she was developing dark spots in each armpit. She wanted to wipe her palms on her thighs, but she knew she'd leave handprints if she did. This was absolutely horrible.

"So, whasup?" Benjamin said into the microphone.

The kids in the audience laughed. Lily glanced at Mrs. Reinhold, who looked as if she'd been shot.

Whasup? Lily thought. *That's how he starts his speech? How did Mrs. Reinhold ever pick him?*

Benjamin grinned at the audience as if he'd gotten away with something, ran his finger under his nose, and then draped himself on the podium and started to talk. Every few phrases he stopped, did the nose thing again, then laughed at himself and went on. Kids in the crowd were spurring him on with laughter and even a few comments. Most of the parents were squirming like they'd like to escape.

Good grief, Lily thought, *hasn't he even practiced it one time since he got picked? He's awful!*

He was so awful, in fact, that it took him a while to find an ending, and one of the judges called time. Mrs. Reinhold had told them if they ran over five minutes, points would he deducted — if Benjamin even had any points left by now.

The applause he received sounded like relief that he was finally getting off the stage. Lily clapped in hopes that it would dry off some of the sweat. She stopped when she realized she was next.

This is it, she thought frantically. *I have to do this. I have to do my best. I have to try to win.*

As Mr. Tanini called her name and her family cheered wildly from the third row, Lily somehow stood up and made her way to the steps that led up to the stage. Her thoughts continued to stumble over themselves.

How can I win now, after Suzy did so well? How can I win when I'm so scared I'm about to throw up?

But another thought crept in among the rest. It said: *You can't be any worse than Benjamin. You're going to look amazing after him—right after him.*

It was enough to get her to the podium and enough to let her look out at all the faces tilted expectantly up toward hers. But there were so many of them. And some of them weren't pulling for her—Suzy's parents weren't—or Zooey—or Zooey's mom.

But there were four somebodies who were—Mom and Dad and Reni and Art. They were all sitting there looking confident, hands folded casually in their laps like they were waiting for the start of a movie they already knew was going to be great.

It was enough to make her smile. And when Art crossed his eyes at her, it made her open her mouth and let the first line come out. The voice she heard was strong and clear. She barely recognized the sound of the girl who spoke for the next four and one half minutes without stumbling even once. She didn't feel like she was Lily again until she left the stage, amid enthusiastic applause.

They're clapping for me! she thought as she took the stairs down. *They thought I was good!*

But even as she caught Reni's eye and saw her give a thumbs-up, Lily knew the clapping wasn't as loud as it had been for Suzy. Mr. Tanini didn't say Lily had set a new standard for the last few speakers. And she didn't feel as happy as Suzy had looked when she'd finished her speech. All she felt was her heart pounding in her chest because at least it was over.

When the last kid had given his speech, Mr. Tanini told the audience they could go out into the lobby for refreshments while the judges tallied their results. He would let them know when to come back in for the announcement of the winners.

Lily was the first one out of her row. She *really* had to go to the bathroom, and she looked straight ahead as she charged up the aisle. Four rows up, she collided head-on with Zooey.

"Sorry!" Lily said. She put both hands on Zooey's shoulders so she wouldn't stumble forward, but Zooey shook away.

""Suzy was great!" Lily blurted out. "I was so proud of her!"

"Why were you proud of her?" Zooey said. "I'm the one who helped her!"

Lily couldn't think of an answer. She knew she was staring at Zooey like an idiot. To her surprise, Zooey suddenly smiled.

"But it's okay," she said, "because she is *so* gonna win."

"I'm sure she'll be one of the winners," Lily said. "There's gonna be two."

"Oh yeah, huh?" Zooey said.

Her gray eyes softened, just for a moment. It was a hopeful moment for Lily, but it passed, and Zooey stepped back. She didn't tell Lily she should go on home now because she wasn't going to be the other winner. She didn't say anything. She just hurried away.

Maybe I don't want to be the winner, Lily thought as she wove through the people toward the lobby. *Not if it means I can't keep my friends.*

"Lily!"

Lily stopped in the doorway in time for Reni to hurl herself at her.

"You were awesome! You're gonna win—I know it!"

Lily clung to Reni and tried not to cry. She still had Reni. That was a lot.

"Nice job, Lil," she heard her mother say. "Very smooth."

"Yeah," Art said. "I didn't even fall asleep."

Dad hugged her, and Lily melted into the smell of his British Sterling and fountain pen ink.

"I was proud of you," he said. "It takes real maturity to go on in spite of nerves."

"You could tell I was nervous?" Lily said.

"You think?" Art said. "You've only been driving us nuts about this for the last week."

"How about that Suzy?" Dad said. "She's a sleeper, isn't she?"

"What does that mean?" Reni said. Her eyes lit up. "Did she put you to sleep?"

"No," Dad said. "It means who would have expected that timid little thing to be such a dynamic speaker?"

"It was pure luck," Reni muttered to Lily.

Just then Kresha burst onto the scene and kissed Lily on each cheek as if she'd already won both slots in the county competition.

"Dude — lighten up," Art said. "It's not the Olympics."

"You do good, Lee-lee," Kresha said. "You hear me cheer?"

"Was that you whistling through your teeth back there?" Mom said.

Kresha nodded, grinning.

"We heard," Mom said.

Dad fished his glasses out of his jacket pocket and put them on to watch Benjamin strut past.

"The next thing they need to do in this school," Dad said, "is teach some audience deportment. An educated audience would have nipped that child's shenanigans in the bud."

"You know he's not gonna win," Reni said.

Kresha hugged Lily around the neck. "More chance for you, Lee-lee," she said.

That didn't make Lily feel a whole lot better. Maybe she could beat Benjamin — and if she didn't she was convinced she'd die — but was she better than everybody else? Had people clapped as much for the other kids as they had for her and she'd been too nervous to notice? Was her family trying to make her feel better?

I hate this, she thought. *I can't stand it—I want it to be over so I don't have to feel like I'm gonna throw up, and I can get my friends back. I want to go home and forget the whole thing!*

"What's up?" Art said to her. "You look kinda green."

"I have to go to the bathroom," Lily said, and she fled.

A few minutes later, when Lily was rinsing out her mouth at the sink, Reni rushed in.

"Come on!" she said. "They're about to announce the winners!"

"Could you just listen and then come tell me?" Lily said. "I'll wait here."

"How about no!" Reni grabbed her hand and pulled her out the door. "I wanna see your face when they call your name."

Lily let Reni drag her back into the auditorium, and she just made it into her seat when Mr. Tanini said, "Ladies and gentlemen—"

He went on for an agonizing two minutes about how proud he and the teachers were of the speakers and how hard it had been for the judges to make a choice. Lily spent that time trying to figure out how to react when she lost so nobody would know she was destroyed.

Finally Mr. Tanini unfolded a piece of paper, made a joke about needing a drumroll, and then said, "I am pleased and proud to announce that our two representatives to the Burlington County Seventh Grade Speech Competition will be—Miss Suzanne Wheeler—"

The audience roared so loudly and for so long that Mr. Tanini had to raise his hand for quiet.

"—and," he said, "Miss Lilianna Robbins. Ladies, congratulations!"

As the auditorium rang with shouts and cheers and clapping and Kresha's whistles, Lily sat dead still in her seat. For all her worrying and sweating and even throwing up, it had never occurred to her that it might be her and Suzy—competing for something even more important. That this was going to go on—that it wasn't over—that in fact the stakes were now higher.

The girl next to Lily said, "Congratulations. You were good."

Lily nodded numbly. All she wanted to do was get out of there so she could think. She even stood up. When she did, Suzy was standing up too, and their eyes met.

Lily knew her eyes were saying, *Suzy, is this as awful for you as it is for me? What are we going to do?*

But Suzy's eyes showed no such confusion. They were shining, dancing, even, as Lily had never seen them do before. She beamed a smile, and then she turned to Zooey, who was climbing over three other people to get to her.

"You did it!" Zooey cried. "And you're going to do it again! You're going to go all the way to nationals!"

It was a sickening thought. Lily sank back into her seat and wished for a barf bag.

Chapter 7

Somehow Lily let the crowd move her to the lobby, where the first person she saw was Mrs. Reinhold. She shook Lily's hand and said matter-of-factly, "I suspected you would move up. You're a hard worker."

"Thank you," Lily said. For some reason, she was blotching up, and she hadn't even embarrassed herself.

"But there is more hard work to come," Mrs. Reinhold said. "I want you and Suzanne to come to my room every day at lunch for the next two weeks so we can continue to polish. There will be only eight contestants at county, but the competition will be very stiff. You want to make a good showing."

"I want to win," Lily said. It came out automatically. *What else do you say at a time like this?* she wondered.

"If you do, and there will be only one winner this time, you will move on to the state contest."

Lily nodded.

"Now go celebrate," Mrs. Reinhold said. "Even if you go no further than county, that's a great accomplishment. Enjoy it a little."

Mrs. Reinhold looked up at Mom and Dad, who were approaching with proud gleams on their faces, and shook their hands. Lily's eyes drifted past them to a scene further out in the lobby.

Suzy was standing there, glowing, while Zooey and Kresha took turns hugging her and practically dancing around her like she was the Maypole. Even Suzy's parents and sisters didn't look as happy as those Girlz did.

Lily didn't feel happy. What she felt was a crushing sadness that she couldn't go over and dance with them. And a stark fear that she had to do all of this again in two weeks. And a hard, cold determination to be the one everybody danced around next time — the only one.

"Lil," Mom said at her side. "Have you congratulated Suzy yet?"

Lily shook her head. "I don't think she wants to talk to me."

"That's not what I asked you. A real winner makes the effort, no matter what response she thinks she'll get."

"Can't I do it later?" Lily said.

"Now is the appropriate time," Mom said.

Lily sighed and went slowly toward Suzy. She decided on the way that this must be what it felt like to walk to the gas chamber. Suzy turned from Zooey to look at Lily, and Lily was sure her smile faded a little. It was all she could do not to run back to Mom and beg to be grounded for a week. Still — if this was part of being a real winner.

"Suzy," Lily said, extending her hand, "I just wanted to say congratulations. You deserved to win."

Suzy looked at Lily's outstretched hand for a second and then stuck hers into it. It felt warm against Lily's cold, still clammy palm. Lily gave it a squeeze — and Suzy at once jerked away.

"Thanks," Suzy said.

"Come *on*, Suzy," Zooey said. "My mom's calling ahead to get us a table." She tugged at Suzy's arm, but her eyes were on Lily "This is gonna be so cool."

"Have fun," Lily said. Her voice came out like a piece of wood, and as she turned away, she felt another piece snap inside of her. It hurt like nothing else.

Mom and Dad were waiting for her when she got back to them. They'd obviously been watching.

"Good for you, Lilliputian," Dad murmured to her.

"It didn't go well?" Mom said.

"No," Lily said.

"Hey, are we going for ice cream or anything?" Art said.

"No," Lily said. "I want to go home."

The minute they got there, Lily wanted to tear upstairs to her room, but before she could even get her coat off, Mom said, "I'm going to check on Joe. Then why don't you come in Dad's study? We need to talk to you."

Lily was already so full of sadness and dread that she didn't see how the night could get any worse, so without argument she hung up her coat and went into the study to wait. A few moments later, Dad appeared in the doorway with a container of ice cream in each hand.

"Rocky Road or mint chocolate chip?" he said.

"I don't care for any," Lily said. "I can't eat at a time like this."

"A time like what?" Mom said from behind him. She pointed to the mint chocolate chip and held up two fingers.

"A time like what?" she said again when Dad had disappeared in the direction of the kitchen.

"Half my friends hate me now!" Lily said. "All because I want to win too!"

Mom perched on the arm of the chair Lily was sitting in. "Your dad and I definitely didn't like what we saw tonight. There wasn't a glimmer of good sportsmanship in that whole room."

"Public speaking's not exactly a sport, Mom," Lily said.

"But it *is* a competition, and the same rules apply," Mom said. "You try to do your best and hope it's better than anybody else's best. When it isn't, you may be sad, but you accept it graciously and admire and learn from the better player's skill."

"Suzy isn't doing that, though!" Lily said. "She's listening to Zooey, and—"

"And who are you listening to?" Mom said.

Lily tucked her hair behind her ears with impatient fingers. "I'm listening to God, Mom. I've been praying about this, like, nonstop."

"I'm sure you have," Mom said.

Dad arrived with a bowl of Rocky Road and a bowl of mint chocolate chip. Both bowls had two spoons.

"Eat," Mom said to Lily. "You're making yourself sick over this whole thing, and you're wasting away to nothing. Pick a flavor and eat."

"Or pick both flavors," Dad said as he perched on the edge of his desk and eyed the Rocky Road. "I'm partial to that one, myself. There's nothing like frozen marshmallows to pick you up."

"I really don't feel like eating," Lily said. She folded her arms. She could feel Mom and Dad exchanging glances over her head.

"Lilliputian," Dad said, "are you sure you want to be a public speaker? Are you sure—"

"I know it's what I'm supposed to do!" Lily said. "Otherwise Mrs. Reinhold wouldn't have picked me for the contest. And then I won again tonight. God wants me to do my best out there—I prayed about it, and I feel it."

"God always wants you to do your best," Dad said. "If I asked you to wash these bowls, God would want you to do your best at it."

Lily tried not to roll her eyes. "I know that," she said, her lips tight.

"God also wants you to take pleasure in the work he gives you to do," Dad said.

"Your father is a living example of that," Mom said. Her lips twitched. "I had to put my foot down about him reading at the dinner table the first week we were married."

Dad set the now half-empty bowl of Rocky Road on the desk and leaned toward Lily.

"My question is," he said, "when do you feel God's pleasure as you're speaking?"

Lily twisted her mouth for a second. "What does that feel like?" she said.

"At what point do you feel like you'd rather be doing this than anything else?" Mom said.

Lily's twist turned into a grin. "When it's over! When I win."

"What's the rest of it like for you?" Dad said.

Lily had to think about that one. "I get really scared beforehand—like throw-up scared. It's about like sitting in the waiting room at the dentist—only worse."

Dad nodded. "I read a study just the other day where they asked people to list their worst fears. The number one fear was speaking in front of a group—and the number two was dying." He grinned. "That shows that the majority of people would rather die than give a speech."

"I know *that* thing," Lily said.

"So why do it, Lil?" Mom said. "Why put yourself through all that agony?"

"Because," Lily said. "I like to win."

There was another exchanging of glances. It made Lily feel squirmy.

"Is that bad?" she said. "I mean, I'm not being evil about it like Zooey is, and Suzy. They don't even want to be friends if I beat Suzy."

"That part does concern us," Dad said. "Although you can't do anything about Suzy's attitude except refuse to take it on yourself."

"Oh—I won't," Lily said.

"But it goes deeper than that," Dad went on. "Your mother and I are not so sure public speaking is what God wants you to pursue—at least, not on a competitive level."

Lily couldn't hold herself back anymore. "You always do this!" she said. "Every time I think I've found my thing that I'm the best at, you guys start criticizing it and telling me to make sure it's a God thing. It's that way with everything I think is fun to do!"

The minute the words were out of her mouth, Lily cringed. That was *so* not the thing to do with Mom and Dad.

But nobody yelled or pointed out the path to her room. Mom and Dad looked at each other yet again, and Dad said, "Fun, Lilliputian? You're telling us the preparation and the nausea and the agony of getting up there in front of all those people is fun for you?"

"No," Lily said. "The fun part is when I win. I don't expect the rest of it to be a blast."

"You should," Mom said. "Do you think I devote eight hours a day, five days a week to something that is agony to me, just so I can maybe have ten seconds of jollies when my team wins?"

"I don't know," Lily said.

"No—I do not. I love the process—the training and the practicing and seeing it all come together. I get as jazzed about every good spike one of my girls makes in practice as I do about bringing home a trophy. Winning is just a sign that you love what you do so much that you want to be the best."

They let her think about that for a minute, but Lily didn't know where to put her thoughts. What she was doing to be the best speaker didn't sound like what Mom did to get her team to win volleyball games. Still—it was so different.

"I want to win because I'm competitive, like you, Mom."

Mom's mouth was twitchless. "Oh—I don't think that sounds like me at all, Lil."

"But why is it bad when I want to compete? Everybody gets all excited when Art wins at contests, and we're all practically in mourning because Joe can't play sports for, like, a month—but if I say I want to win at something, we have to sit down and talk about it like I'm doing something wrong." Lily felts her eyes narrowing. "Is it because I'm a girl?"

Mom closed her eyes. "Don't you even go there with me, Lilianna."

"Okay," Dad said quickly, "let's see where we are. Lily—your mother and I are concerned that your reasons for pursuing these speech contests are not reasons that are going to lead you where God wants you to go. Now I know how easy it is to come up with a plan and then ask God to bless it. We've talked about that before. We have no doubt that you're praying, but be sure you're asking God what *he* wants you to do—and be sure you're listening."

"Okay," Lily said. "I'm not arguing or being a smart-mouth with you or anything, but I have to ask this."

"Go for it," Mom said.

"If God doesn't want me to do this, how come I keep winning?"

"Let me ask *you* a question," Mom said. "If God wants you to do this, why are your friends turning away from you?" Mom put her hand up. "I'm not saying it's right for Suzy and Zooey to behave the way they have. In fact, I'd like to shake both of them. But do you see what I'm saying? You need to ask God what's important for you to do—and ask him for the right signs."

"Not whether you're winning," Dad said, "but whether winning is bringing pleasure to you and him and the people around you—and whether the process of getting the win makes you a better person."

"Isn't my winning bringing you guys pleasure?" Lily said. "Like when Joe's soccer team won the county championship and you bought the whole team pizza?"

Nobody answered for a few seconds. That was an answer as far as Lily was concerned.

"We are very, very proud of you," Dad said finally. "It takes a lot of courage to do what you did tonight. But pleasure—for me?" He shook his head. "That was one of the most nerve-wracking evenings I've ever spent." He grinned and picked up the bowl of Rocky Road. "That's why I'm rewarding myself. I highly recommend it."

"Come on, Lil," Mom said. "Don't let me eat this whole bowl. I'll hate myself in the morning. Grab a spoon."

But Lily stood up. "I'm not hungry," she said. "Can I go to bed now?"

Dad's eyes got soft. "Don't think we aren't proud of you, because we are."

"I know," Lily said. "Can I go?"

When they nodded, she left at a stiff walk.

You're gonna be even prouder of me when I win at county, she thought as she took the stairs. *You're gonna see—*

As she wrote fast and furiously in her God journal, the determined vision of herself graciously accepting the county award took center stage. Gone—at least for the moment—was the pathetic scene of her practically begging Suzy to hug her and say they were friends again and Suzy coldly turning away.

She could envision herself walking across the stage, head held high to embrace the warm handshake of the county superintendent of schools. She could see the pride in his eyes, hear the enthusiastic support of everyone in the audience, even the parents of the speakers who had lost. She could almost taste success at its best.

Lily closed her eyes then and tried to feel the pleasure of it. She could definitely feel the excitement and relief pulsing through her veins—that felt good. But pleasure?

"I'll feel really good if Suzy is out there giving me a standing ovation too," Lily said to Otto. "I gotta pray that God will work on that."

But that didn't sound like the way Dad had told her to pray. He'd said she needed to ask God to lead her where he wanted her to go.

Lily closed her eyes, but they flew open again. It was too scary to go there—to a place where God didn't want her to win. The vision of having to stand up and clap for somebody else while her stomach sank like a stone was so dark and sad she couldn't even think it.

That wouldn't give God pleasure, she thought. *I know it.*

Lily was a little later than usual getting to school the next morning, but there was no one at the bench. She headed straight to her locker, wondering as she went whether most winners felt this bummed out the morning after winning a big prize.

She was wallowing so deeply in that thought that she didn't notice at first that there was a piece of paper stuck in the crack around her locker. She looked around, but no one else appeared to have a flier. People weren't supposed to do that anyway—Mr. Tanini said they always ended up all over the floor.

Lily shifted her backpack, unfolded the paper, and then took in a sharp breath.

Someone had cut words out of magazines and pasted them to the paper to form a warning:

DO YOURSELF A FAVOR. DROP OUT OF THE COUNTY
CONTEST. YOU CAN'T WIN ANYWAY.
SUZY W. IS GOING TO RUN AWAY WITH IT.

Lily had seen cutout letters on ransom notes in movies, and they always gave her the creeps. This one sent cold chills from her neck to her tailbone. She dropped the note and stared down at it.

This is evil! she thought. *Even for Ashley!* All this drama for a moron like Benjamin?

Lily's thought train screeched to a halt. Benjamin? He wasn't even in the running anymore. Of course, Ashley and her friends probably didn't know that, since they weren't there—although Benjamin surely would have called them.

Lily picked up the paper and studied it. *Suzy W. is going to run away with it,* it said. Ashley and her friends wouldn't want Suzy to win.

'Course, they do hate my guts, Lily thought. *They'd root for Suzy if it meant I'd lose.*

Lily could feel her heart getting heavy. With Benjamin out of the competition, why would they even care? Did they hate her that much?

I don't care! she told herself firmly. *I have to concentrate on winning at county. That's what matters. Mom and Dad, Suzy and Zooey — everybody's gonna see that this is what I'm meant to do. It's my one chance to be a winner at something.*

So she focused her mind on that and the first step in accomplishing it — the coaching session with Mrs. Reinhold during lunch. Lily snatched her brown bag from her locker after fourth period and hurried to get to Mrs. R.'s room before Suzy, just to show how eager she was. Suzy was already there, sitting primly at a desk with only an apple in front of her. Lily stuffed her lunch under the desk and sat down.

"You ladies may eat while I review last night's speeches for you," Mrs. Reinhold said.

Suzy disregarded the apple, so Lily folded her hands and forgot about the turkey on wheat in her bag. Whatever Suzy did, she could do it better, she decided.

"Lilianna," Mrs. Reinhold said, peering at her notes through her small glasses. "You are very fluent, which means you seldom hesitate over a word —"

Lily scrambled for her backpack so she could get out pencil and paper to take notes. Suzy reached into the pocket of her jacket and pulled out a pad and pen. Lily made a mental note to be more prepared tomorrow.

"Mrs. Reinhold?" Lily said. "When *did* I hesitate over a word?"

"Excuse me?"

"You said I seldom hesitate over a word, but when *did* I? Seldom doesn't mean never."

Mrs. Reinhold considered her notes. "All right, Lilianna, I suppose you *never* hesitate over a word — at least you didn't last night."

Lily beamed and resisted the urge to look at Suzy to see how she was reacting.

"You look quite poised in spite of your nervousness, Lilianna—"

"How could you tell I was nervous?" Lily said.

Mrs. Reinhold raised an eyebrow. "Let me give you all the positive strokes first, Lilianna. Then we'll discuss how you can improve."

"Good," Lily said.

"I'm glad you approve. Now—your volume is excellent and your articulation very clear. Of course, you know the speech backward and forward—I saw no lapses of memory. Decent eye contact."

She stopped. Lily looked up, pen positioned over her list.

"I'm ready," Lily said.

"That's all. In the next two weeks, we are going to work on facial expression and more audience connection. You're still rather stiff. We want you to be poised but not so formal that you look like a robot."

"I look like a robot?" Lily said. This was not good. Suzy had definitely not looked like a robot.

"Perhaps that's a bit of an exaggeration," Mrs. Reinhold said. "Let's just say we're going to loosen you up."

Lily wiggled her shoulders. "I can do loose," she said.

Mrs. Reinhold nodded and turned to Suzy, who, it appeared, had been writing down all of the notes Mrs. Reinhold had given Lily.

Why is she writing down my stuff? Lily thought.

She didn't know, but she decided to write down Suzy's. She drew a line down the center of her paper and wrote Suzy/Good, Suzy/Bad at the tops of the columns.

"Suzanne, you amazed me," Mrs. Reinhold said. "I thought your speech here in the classroom was excellent, but you surpassed even that last night. You like having a real audience, don't you?"

"I was nervous," Suzy said.

"Not once you got past your first sentence, if it even took you that long," Mrs. Reinhold said. "You warmed to the audience, and they in turn warmed to you. I was also impressed by—"

Lily was having a hard time keeping up with all the compliments Mrs. Reinhold was giving Suzy. By the time she got to the things Suzy needed to work on, Lily had a cramp in her hand. That didn't turn out to be a problem, because there was only one thing to write in the Suzy/Bad column.

"We're going to work on your pre-speech and post-speech behaviors," Mrs. Reinhold said. "Should the judges see you before the contest and notice your body language as you're going back to your seat after the speech, they may be unduly influenced by how meek and timid you seem."

But she is meek and timid! Lily wanted to shout. *Can't you see that?*

She looked down at the lists, the one she'd written down for herself and the one for Suzy. Maybe Mrs. Reinhold didn't see that, because while she'd given Lily five compliments, Suzy had received ten.

Nausea seized Lily again. Suzy was already ahead, and they'd barely started.

Chapter
8

The next week was one of the hardest in Lily's life so far. So many things seemed to be going against her.

In the first place, she felt uncomfortable around Mom and Dad, knowing that they didn't quite understand about her need to win. It didn't seem to bother them that Art wanted to win. He practiced his college audition piece on his saxophone every night for hours while Lily was trying to practice her speech for Otto in the room below.

"There's no point in complaining to Mom and Dad about the noise," she told Otto one night. He, as usual, had his paws over his ears. "They'll just say it's important for him to practice so he can get a scholarship. *My* need to practice is, of course, chopped liver."

To make matters worse, Joe was so down in the dumps about not being able to play sports for six weeks that he was almost impossible to live with. He flipped channels until Lily was sure his thumb must ache, and he ate every snack food in the kitchen — not that Lily really cared about that. She was so nervous all the time, she couldn't even think about eating — which made dinner times a little tense. While Art was offering to eat her share, Mom and Dad were practically force-feeding her.

"It wasn't this hard to get you to eat when you were five," Mom said. "Although I think the reason you didn't clean your plate then was because you didn't stop talking long enough."

Dad chuckled. "I used to say, 'Take five bites, and then you can say something.'"

"Yeah," Art said, "so she'd stuff five spoonfuls in and then talk with it squirting out all over."

"I did not!" Lily said.

"Yeah—I think you did, Lil," Mom said.

So much for family support, Lily thought.

She did get support from Reni. But as much as she wanted to win the speech contest, Lily got a little annoyed with Reni at times. Winning seemed to be *all* Reni could talk about.

One day it was, "Lil, we gotta work on your confidence. If you tell yourself you might lose, you probably will. Don't even think about that."

Another day, it was, "Are you gonna do your nails? They'll be able to see your hands—you better do your nails."

Passing the bakery prompted Reni to say, "When you win state, we should get your celebration cake there."

Going to the movies together on Friday night was cause for, "Watch the actors' facial expressions. Then you'll see what Mrs. Reinhold means."

Saturday morning, after they had spent the night together Friday night, the first words on Reni's lips when she woke up were, "Only seven more days 'til the competition, Lil. You are *so* gonna win."

Lily wasn't getting that kind of support from anybody else except Kresha—and even she was torn between Lily and Suzy, so Lily didn't tell Reni that she wished she'd lighten up. Besides, there were other things that bothered her more—like the magazine cutout messages she got stuffed in her locker every day.

One of them said:

> YOU REALLY DON'T GET IT, DO YOU?
> YOU AREN'T GOING TO WIN.
> GIVE IT UP.

Another one said:

> WHAT ARE YOU, NUTS?
> YOU CAN'T BEAT SUZY WHEELER.
> SO FORGET IT.

A third told her:

> YOU ARE THE LOSER.
> SUZY IS THE WINNER.
> GET A CLUE.

Reni was with Lily when she discovered the fourth one of the week. She snatched it out of Lily's hand and read aloud:

> TOMORROW IS SUZY'S BIG DAY.
> GET OUT WHILE YOU CAN
> BEFORE YOU EMBARASS YOURSELF.

Reni grunted. "Whoever it is misspelled 'embarrass.' They obviously aren't in Mrs. Reinhold's class."

"They are, though," Lily said. "Ashley—Chelsea—Bernadette—Benjamin."

"You still think it's them?"

"Who else?" Lily said. "Just throw that in the trash, okay? I have to get to Mrs. Reinhold's. Me and Suzy have to give our speeches to each other and critique the other person's."

"Let her have it," Reni said.

"You really think I should do that?" Lily said.

"Well—be honest. But don't, like, be all nice and think you're gonna hurt her feelings telling her about something that *is* wrong."

"Mrs. Reinhold says we have to critique in the form of suggestions."

"So suggest that she get a life," Reni said. She tossed the now balled-up note into a trash can. "See you fifth period."

She left, and Lily was about to hurry toward Mrs. Reinhold's room when someone stepped into her path.

"Hey," Shad Shifferdecker said.

"Hey," Lily said.

"I seen you getting them letters in your locker," he said, moving his right shoulder and pointing his finger downward. It was what all the boys who wore their pants hanging down below the elastic on their boxer shorts always did. Supposedly it was cool.

"So—" Lily said carefully.

"So—I also heard you and the black chick readin' it out loud."

"Her name is Reni," Lily said.

"Yeah—her. I can never remember—weird name."

"I really hafta go," Lily said.

She started to go around him, but he backed up and put the palms of his hands up in front of him. "Whoa."

"What?"

"You think it's Ashley and them's been doin' it. It ain't them."

"Who else would do it? They hate me, okay? It's *so* them."

"Nope," Shad said. He pushed a finger under his nose.

"Then who?"

"You don't wanna know, trust me."

"Then why did you even bring it up? You're just saying that because you don't want me to bust Ashley and them."

"I don't care if you bust them," Shad said. "They ain't no friends a mine."

73

"You used to go out with Ashley."

"I also used to pick my nose," Shad said. "But I broke that habit too."

"Gross me out and make me icky!"

"Pretty much."

Shad grinned, the familiar evil glint in his eyes. Lily rolled hers.

"So you're saying it isn't Ashley's crowd that's leaving me hate notes. It's somebody else, but you aren't gonna tell me who."

"Right."

"So why are we having this conversation?"

Shad shrugged inside his too-big shirt. "You just gotta watch your back, that's all," he said. "You never know who's gonna take a bite outta you."

"Lovely," Lily said. "I gotta go."

"Yeah—Mrs. R.—she gets bent outta shape when you're late."

It didn't strike Lily until she was almost inside Mrs. Reinhold's room that Shad had known where she was going. But she didn't have a clue how he could have known, and she didn't have time to think about it. She had to do her speech for Suzy.

In the time they'd been working with Mrs. Reinhold, they hadn't worked on their speeches that much, though she'd encouraged them to practice at home. Mostly they'd done some pretty wild exercises to improve their voices, posture, and facial expressions. It had been the one fun part of the whole ugly pre-contest period, and Lily had enjoyed it. It involved a lot of making faces and funny noises, and she and Suzy had giggled at the same time on a number of occasions.

On those occasions, they'd looked at each other, eyes still smiling, before they looked away. Several times, Lily wanted to grab Suzy's shoulders and say, "Suzy, can't we still be friends?" She even planned to say something to her the minute the bell rang at the end of lunch, but every day the door flew open and Zooey came in to whisk Suzy away, with only a backward glare at Lily. After the fourth day, Lily gave up on the idea.

Today Lily barely slid into her seat before the bell rang. Suzy, of course, was already there, note cards stacked neatly on her desk, looking composed, the way Mrs. Reinhold had told her she should look before she was called on.

"Good, Lilianna, you're here," Mrs. Reinhold said. "Why don't you go first?"

Lily straightened her shoulders, trying to look more composed than Suzy, and stepped up to the podium. She looked directly at Suzy and smiled, just as Mrs. Reinhold had taught her to do. Then she began.

It was the easiest speech she had ever given. Her palms weren't sweaty yet, and she could control the tremble in her voice. Of course, there weren't two hundred people in the room—there was only Suzy—and she listened as if she were savoring every word that came out of Lily's mouth.

Even as she laid out her lines perfectly, Lily was able to think, *Suzy's enjoying my speech. She likes listening to me!*

When she was finished, Lily didn't feel like running for the nearest restroom, and Suzy clapped, a little more than politely.

"Much improved, Lilianna," Mrs. Reinhold said. "Any comments, Suzanne?"

Suzy sat up straighter in her seat and looked up at Mrs. Reinhold. "She had good eye contact—I liked that," she said.

"Tell it to Lilianna," Mrs. Reinhold said. "This is just two friends having a conversation about their speeches."

The words grabbed at Lily as Suzy slowly turned toward her.

"I liked your eye contact," Suzy said. "You looked right at me the whole time."

And you're looking at me! Lily wanted to cry. *You're looking at me and talking to me!*

"Anything else?" Mrs. Reinhold said.

"Oh—yeah—there's a lot of stuff!" Suzy said. "She—" Suzy turned back to Lily. "I mean, *you* didn't look nervous like usual. You looked like you were relaxed and meant what you were saying—"

She kept going until Mrs. Reinhold said, "All right—any suggestions for Lilianna, Suzanne?"

Suzy tilted her head in thought, and Lily held her breath. Finally Suzy said, "I just suggest you do it exactly that way at the contest. It was your best ever."

Mrs. Reinhold, of course, added a few more suggestions, but Lily hardly heard them. It felt so good to have Suzy talking to her again, she couldn't think about anything else.

Not until Mrs. Reinhold said, "All right, Suzanne, your turn."

Then Lily turned her focus on Suzy and listened and watched with rapt attention as her friend gave her speech. Suzy talked right to her with such expression that a few times Lily forgot Suzy was giving a speech. When Suzy finished her last line, Lily clapped.

"Spontaneous applause," Mrs. Reinhold said to Suzy. "The most genuine of compliments."

"But I have a lot more compliments," Lily said. "Suzy—you are awesome. You give a speech like you're just, like, talking to somebody, only it's polished up—"

She went on until the first warning bell rang. Suzy was glowing, and Mrs. Reinhold was nodding her head in approval.

"I'm very pleased with the work you two have done," she said. "I know you will both be winners tomorrow."

"But I thought there was only one winner in this contest," Lily said.

"One contest winner," Mrs. Reinhold said. "But that isn't the kind of winner I'm talking about."

The last bell rang then, and she shooed them toward the door. "Get a good night's sleep. Tomorrow will be stressful. You know where to go—the high school Little Theatre."

Suzy and Lily nodded until Mrs. Reinhold finally turned back to her desk. Then Lily grinned at Suzy.

"I think she's more nervous than we are," she whispered.

Suzy giggled as Lily pushed open the door. For once, Zooey wasn't there.

"You want to walk to fifth period with me?" Lily said.

She held her breath. Suzy gave her a long look and then said, "Sure."

They took a few steps down the hall, side by side, and Lily searched for something to say, something to keep them walking together. It was Suzy who found the words first.

"Did you get all that math homework?" she said. "I didn't understand half the problems."

"Art helped me!" Lily said. She was so grateful they were talking that she let it fly with double exclamation points. "My stuff's in my locker. Come with me, and I'll show you how to do it before class."

Suzy's face stiffened. "You're going to your locker?" she said.

"Yeah," Lily said. "I have to."

"Oh," Suzy said. Her eyes darted around as if she were looking for the rescue squad. "Well—I'll just meet you in class."

Then without another word, she hurried off, nearly plowing down a kid who was carrying a large science project.

Lily's heart sank.

I really thought we were getting somewhere, she said to herself. *What did I say wrong this time?*

She watched Suzy fade into the hall mob and then headed for her locker. When she got there, she stopped at the end of the row, and her heart sank even further, stopping with a thud in the pit of her stomach.

There was a white piece of paper sticking out.

"Not another one," Lily said out loud.

"You want me to get 'em for you?" said a voice behind her. "I know who done it. I can kick some tail."

77

Lily didn't even turn toward Shad. She just elbowed past the kids who were still at their lockers and pulled out the paper. Shad snatched it from her.

"Why you even wanna look at it?" he said. "You'll just start bawlin' or somethin'."

Lily snatched it back, but she didn't unfold it.

"How do you know?" she said. "Did you already read it?"

"No—but I seen the look on the chick's face when she stuck it in there. She's really got it in for you."

"Ashley?" Lily said.

"I already told you, it ain't her." Shad grunted. "Besides, she's too lazy to go to the trouble of cuttin' out all them little letters and pastin' 'em on there. She'd just tell you to your face."

"Then who is it?"

"You don't wanna know. Just say the word, and I'll get her for you." Shad puffed out his chest. "She'll leave you alone."

Lily tried to look nonchalant. "She—whoever it is—hasn't really done anything to me," she said. "It's just a bunch of words."

"Yeah?" Shad said. "Then how come you look like you're about to hurl?"

"I am *not* about to hurl!"

"Yeah, you are. You wanna go right over to that trashcan and toss your cookies."

"Gross!"

"Could be. Depends what you had for lunch."

Lily flounced past him and twirled the numbers on her locker.

"So—you want me to nail this chick that wants you to lose or what?" Shad said.

Lily pulled open the locker door and groped for her math book.

"It doesn't matter—whatever," she said.

"Okay. Suit yourself. I'd want her tail kicked if a so-called friend of mine ever done that to me, that's all."

Shad sauntered off. Lily froze with one hand on her locker door.

A friend? A friend of mine is doing this?

No way. Shad was just making things up to feel important. Though why he should bother was beyond her. Lily shook her head and headed for the math room.

It doesn't matter, she tried to tell herself. Not only had she just given her best speech ever and not only was she ready to go in and win that county contest tomorrow, but it looked like she and Suzy might be making up.

If we could just convince Zooey, Lily thought. *Then we could all be back together again—better than before because now we're all even going to the same church.*

That lifted her heart up out of her stomach. She reached fifth period just as the bell rang and sat down immediately to write a Girlz-Gram to Suzy: *Let's get in the same group for going over homework. Then I can help you.*

Mr. Chester was taking roll, so Lily was able to pass the note safely to Suzy. When she'd read it, to Lily's relief, Suzy nodded at her.

Reni poked Lily in the back. "Are you guys, like, getting along now?" she whispered.

"I hope so," Lily whispered back. And the minute Mr. Chester told them to form groups, Lily made a beeline for Suzy's corner of the room.

"You have fifteen minutes," Mr. Chester called out over the din.

"Who's got a pencil?" Marcie McCleary said as she dropped into the desk next to Lily.

"Rats," Lily said. She'd been in such a hurry to get over there she'd left hers at her seat.

"Don't worry," Suzy said. "I have plenty."

She opened her binder and flipped back to the front where Lily knew she kept her zippered case full of finely sharpened pencils, all with perfect erasers. Lily leaned over to look—just because it had been a while since she'd last been inspired by Suzy's neatness. When she did, she caught sight of something that turned her blood cold.

Through the clear plastic pencil case, Lily could plainly see several dozen letters and words clipped neatly from magazines. And there, lined up with the pencils, was a small container of glue.

No! Lily almost screamed. *No, Suzy, tell me it wasn't you! Please tell me!*

But Suzy turned from handing Marcie a pencil just in time to catch Lily staring at the pencil case. Her eyes came up and met Lily's. It was a painful moment that shot right through Lily's chest.

"Suzy?" she whispered. "Are you the one?"

Suzy slapped the binder closed, but it was too late. The answer was clear in her eyes. She was the one. She'd been the one all along.

Chapter 9

Lily asked Mr. Chester for a pass to the restroom, and she stayed there, crying and trying not to throw up, until Reni flew in.

"Mr. Chester sent me down to see if you were okay," Reni said. She squinted at Lily. "You're not. You look awful."

"I *am* awful!" Lily said.

She sagged against the sink.

"What's going on?" Reni said.

"It's too awful!"

"Would you quit bein' all Drama Queen and tell me? I'm dying here!"

Lily told her the story—from how well things had gone at practice during lunch to her seeing the evidence in Suzy's binder.

"What's she carrying it around with her for?" Reni said. "That's pretty stupid!"

"That's not the point!"

"Man, this stinks!" Reni fingered one of her beaded braids. "Maybe you oughta let Shad take care of her for you—her *and* Zooey."

"Reni!"

"Well, maybe you should."

"No!"

Lily turned to lean over the sink and cry some more.

Reni rubbed her back. "Come on, Lil, you're gonna look all puffy for your speech tomorrow."

"I'm not going."

"Now *you're* being stupid! You gotta go! If you don't, then her little plan worked. You don't want that—you don't want her thinking that she scared you off! You gotta show her you're better than she is."

Lily shook her head.

"Lily!" Reni stopped rubbing and smacked Lily in the back of the head. It didn't hurt—there was way too much hair back there—but it got Lily's attention.

"Knock this off!" Reni said. "If you don't go, she'll probably win. And she doesn't deserve it—not if she has to do this kinda stuff."

"You think?" Lily said.

"I *know*!" Reni said. "Trust me—if you let her think she can win by threatening people and freaking them out, she'll always do it. You gotta stop her by goin' in there and kickin' some tail."

Lily stood up straight and hooked her hair behind her ears. Reni yanked a paper towel out of the dispenser so she could wipe her eyes.

"You gotta show 'em, Lil," she said. "This is bad. You gotta show 'em. Now blow your nose and let's get back before Mr. Chester comes in here lookin' for us."

Lily honked into the paper towel and followed Reni back to fifth period. She was relieved that all the students were at their desks working on that night's homework so she didn't have to go back to the group with Suzy. As soon as class was over, Lily made for the door and scooted down the hall to avoid her. She did miss Suzy, but she ran right into Kresha, who was headed for the same science class she was in sixth period. All the Girlz were in there, in fact, except Zooey.

"Lee-lee!" Kresha said. She grabbed Lily by the backpack and pulled her close so she could examine Lily's face. "You been crying? Vhat?"

Lily was too beaten down to pussyfoot around. "Were you in on it too, Kresha?" she said.

"In vhat? I do not understand."

"Those evil notes I've been getting about the speech contest. Suzy was the one who did it—did you help her?"

Kresha looked down at the scuffed toes of her boots.

"You did!" Lily cried.

"I do not help," Kresha said. "But I know." She looked at Lily, eyes begging. "I vill not help, Lee-lee. Dat wrong!"

"But you should've told me!" Lily said.

Kresha shook her head. "I vill not take the sides. I love everybody."

She looked as if she were being pulled in two directions by a pair of tractors. Lily had to nod. She had to say, "It's okay, Kresha. I understand."

But as they beat the bell into sixth-period science and took their seats, Lily didn't feel okay.

She still betrayed me, Lily thought. *She's wrong. She should have taken my side.*

It was all she could do to get through sixth period. Every time she thought about it—and it was *all* she could think about—she started to cry. Every time she caught a glimpse of Suzy going up to Mr. Nutting's desk or walking to the pencil sharpener, she wanted to throw up. Finally she asked Mr. Nutting if she could go to the restroom. He sent her to the nurse, who told her to lie down with a cold washcloth on her forehead.

Ten minutes later, Mom was there.

"How'd you know?" Lily said.

"Nurse Ratchet in there is a friend of mine," Mom said. "She called and told me my kid looked like she had a virus." Mom smoothed Lily's hair back and looked into her eyes. "Looks like a bad case of contestitis to me."

"It's not just the contest, Mom," Lily said. She told Mom everything that had happened, between choking sobs and several more nose blows. When she wound the story down, she threw her arms around Mom's neck and stayed there until she finished crying—at least for the moment.

"Don't you think this has gone far enough?" Mom said.

Lily pulled back. "You want me to drop out of the contest? Now?"

"No—not at all. What I'm talking about is that it's time you figured out exactly why this contest means so much to you so you can go in there tomorrow with some perspective. You *and* Suzy have let this get way out of control."

"I already told you guys a million times," Lily said. "I want to win—just the way you like your team to win and Joe always has to be on the championship team and Art has to win all these scholarships—"

Mom was shaking her head. "It's not the same, Lil," she said. "I want you to talk to your brothers tonight and hear what they have to say about why they compete."

Lily shook *her* head. "It's not gonna make me feel better, Mom. Suzy still did something really bad to me, and Kresha knew but she didn't tell me. Reni's the only real friend I have left—and she's telling me to go in there and show Suzy who's the best."

"Talk to Joe and Art," Mom said.

"Are you not going to let me be in the contest if I don't?"

"I want you to be in the contest," Mom said. "I just want you to be in the right frame of mind." She pushed a stray curl off of Lily's forehead. "I want this to be the best possible experience for you, Lil, and so far I don't think it has been. Let's see if we can salvage some of this, okay? Talk to your brothers."

Lily secretly hoped Joe would be asleep when she got home, but he was hopping all over the first floor on his crutches, bored out of his skull.

When Lily said, "I'm supposed to talk to you," he said he would do it only if she served him Hot Pockets and grape juice.

When they were finally spread out with the picnic on Joe's bed in the family room, Lily said, "How come you're so freaked out because you can't play sports right now?"

"Because it's fun," Joe said, blowing impatiently on a Hot Pocket that was steaming up into his face. "'Cause, like, if I'm not playin' hockey or soccer or something, I'm totally bored."

"What about the competition?" Lily said.

Joe shrugged. "That's what's fun. It's not a real game unless somebody wins and somebody loses."

"But you get so bummed out when you lose."

"So? Everybody does. Everybody likes to win."

Lily pounced on that. "So you *do* like to win, and *that's* why you play."

Joe suddenly tossed the uneaten Hot Pocket on the paper plate and looked glumly at it.

"I wish I could play right now and lose every game," he said. "If I could just play." When he looked up from the melted cheese, Lily was surprised to see tears in his eyes. "Mom and Dad are gonna make me pick only two sports a year 'cause that stupid doctor said I was already stressin' out my joints playin' year round."

"Oh," Lily said. "And you would hate that."

"I *do* hate it. It's not fair! All the other guys'll be out there playin', and I'll be sittin' around watchin' like some loser."

"You're not a loser, though," Lily said. "It's not your fault you got hurt."

"I just wanna play, that's all," Joe said. He pushed the plate toward Lily. "I'm not that hungry anymore," he said. Then he rolled over and closed his eyes.

Lily felt sorry she'd ever brought it up. She was taking both plates into the kitchen when she ran into Art. She considered forgetting the

85

whole thing, but Art wasn't one to burst into tears, so she said, "Can we talk?"

Art pulled his head out of the refrigerator. He had a head of lettuce in one hand and a bottle of French dressing in the other.

"What's up?" he said. "You got man trouble?"

"No," Lily said. "I just have to ask you a question. Why do you like to compete so much—and do you, like, hate it when you don't get first place?"

Art broke open the lettuce over the sink and wiggled his eyebrows. "Hmm. Let me think. Oh yeah—because every woman loves a winner."

"Oh," Lily said.

"Nah—that's not it. I'm not even dating right now. It got too complicated."

"But what about winning?" Lily said. "Why *do* you like to win?"

Art put the two lettuce halves in a bowl and chopped at them with a knife. He waited until he'd emptied the bottle of French dressing onto it before he answered—and then only after he'd taken a couple of mouthfuls.

"It used to be all about ego," he said finally. "I had to win so I could be first and everybody could see how great a musician I was."

"Is that bad?" Lily said.

"Can be. It was for me. I was a conceited little snot in middle school. Then—remember when I was a freshman and I got picked for All-State band, which, like, no freshman ever did, and about a week before we were supposed to leave I got that big ol' honkin' fever blister on my lip and couldn't play?"

Lily didn't remember it all that clearly, but she nodded. Better not to stop him while he was on a roll.

Art stuffed another forkful of dressing-covered lettuce into his mouth and talked with a bulging cheek.

"It healed up just in time for me to go—but the kid who was my alternate was practicing hard, and I thought I was doomed." He shook his head as he chewed noisily. "Right then I realized my ability to play was completely in God's control—not mine."

"You think God zapped you with a fever blister so you couldn't play?"

"That's not the point. The point is that I realized my gift could be ripped away from me any minute. As long as I have it, I have to be using it for God and give him the credit—*and* I have to accept whatever happens that's out of my control. I've been trying to tell Joe that, but he doesn't get it yet."

Lily wasn't sure she got it either. "So you play for God?" she said.

"Yeah. Well—I mean—I compete for scholarships so I can get into a good music school. I want to get into a good school so I can learn to be good and do some good stuff for God. I'm thinking I might want to compose—y'know, Christian music—maybe a whole musical." He pulled his finger around the now empty inside of the bowl and stuck it in his mouth.

"You just ate an entire head of lettuce," Lily said.

"Gotta keep up my strength," he said. "Anything else? I gotta get back to school for pep band."

After he left, Lily sat thinking at the table until Mom came in, with Dad right behind her.

"Sorry we're late, hon," Mom said. "I bet you kids are starving. We got hung up at the adoption agency. What do you want for dinner?"

"How about a big salad?" Dad said. "Put some of that leftover chicken on top. I like it when you do that."

"You okay, Lil?" Mom said. "Feeling any better?"

"I heard you had a rough time today," Dad said. He sat down at the table next to Lily and put her hand between his two long-fingered ones. "You took a pretty tough shot."

"I'm better," Lily said.

"Did you talk to your brothers?" Mom said. She opened the refrigerator and peered into the veggie drawer. "I could have sworn I bought a head of lettuce."

"Art ate it," Lily said.

"So you did talk to him."

"Give us your conclusions, Lilliputian," Dad said.

"Nix on the salad," Mom said. "What's your second choice?"

"Make that chicken thing — where you pour the orange sauce on it."

Mom went back to the refrigerator, and Dad looked at Lily.

"Joe competes because he loves to play," Lily said. "And Art competes so he can do his best work for God."

Dad nodded thoughtfully. Mom stepped back to get a clearer look at the contents of the refrigerator door.

"I know I also bought a whole big bottle of French dressing," she said.

"He ate that too," Lily said.

"I think those are the right conclusions," Dad said.

"I'm ordering pizza," Mom said, and went for the phone.

Dad grinned at Lily. "I like that conclusion too. Now — what does your research tell you about yourself and why *you* want to win?"

Lily put her face in her hands. "I don't know," she said.

Dad pulled her hands away. The look he gave her was almost stern.

"It's important that you find out, then," he said. "As bright and aggressive as you are, you're going to be put into situations like this over and over again in your life. If you don't get the God view of it, you're going to make a lot of mistakes and experience a lot of hurt. So let's straighten up and take a look at this thing."

Mom hung up the phone. "Pepperoni and extra cheese. Thirty minutes," she said. She sat across from Lily. "Where are we?" she said.

"We're just about to get to the good stuff," Dad said. He rubbed his hands together. "So are you like Joe? Do you love the game?"

"What game?" Lily said.

"Speaking competitively. Do you love every minute of it?"

Lily didn't have to think long before she shook her head.

"No," she said. "I kind of hate it."

"Ding! Correct answer!" Dad said. "And, Lilliputian, it shows. Now, don't misunderstand me—you are a very strong, very impressive speaker. But it's obvious that you aren't having a good time up there."

"Who is?" Lily said.

Mom and Dad looked at each other.

"Who?" Lily said.

"Suzy," Mom said. "Once she gets up there, she has the time of her life. She loves it."

"But she gets so nervous!"

"Everybody does," Dad said. "You speak in *spite* of your nervousness. Suzy forgets to *be* nervous when she gets going. The audience can tell."

"Now, how about Art?" Mom said. "Do you compete for the same reason Art does—because he knows playing music is what God wants him to do?"

"You mean, do I think God wants me to be a speaker?" Lily said. "Yes. I'm winning, aren't I?"

Dad's eyes got softer as he leaned toward her. "This is a hard thing for me to say, Lil, but you've won because you're one of the best they have—and some of the others are pretty bad."

"You're certainly better than the average twelve-year-old," Mom put in.

"You're definitely a strong speaker, and I'm so glad you're having this experience," Dad said. "But if you're doing it just to win at something, this isn't your gift, or at least it doesn't appear to be at this point."

89

They were both quiet while Lily thought. She waited to feel stung or like she'd been punched in the stomach, but that didn't happen. In fact, she felt kind of relieved. And then a bad thought grabbed her.

"So tomorrow," she said, "all the really best, gifted kids are gonna be there, and I'm gonna look like a loser compared to them."

Dad made a buzzing sound. "Wrong," he said. "You're a strong speaker. You'll make a good showing."

"But I won't win."

"Maybe not," Dad said. "At least, not in the sense of getting a trophy and moving up to the state level."

Lily looked helplessly at Mom.

"What he means is, you might not win first place, but you *can* be a winner in another way."

"What other way is there?" Lily asked.

The doorbell rang.

"You get the pizza," Dad said to Mom, "and I'll grab my Bible. Lilliputian, make a path in the family room so we can get in there."

The Bible? Lily thought as she collected plates, cups, and empty popcorn bags from around the bed where Joe was sleeping. *We're gonna look up something in the Bible now?*

That wasn't so unusual in the Robbins' house. They looked up stuff and talked about Bible things a lot. Lily just couldn't see how it was going to help her in this situation. But if it could clear up some of the confusion in her head, she was all for it.

Joe slept through the whole dinner and discussion, though Mom was careful to save him about half a pizza for later. The three of them sat on the floor near his bed and ate the stringy cheese and pepperoni while Dad read about Jesus and his disciples from Mark 9. *"What were you arguing about on the road?"* But they kept quiet because on the way they had argued about who was the greatest. Sitting down, Jesus called *the Twelve and said, "If anyone wants to be first, he must be the very last, and the servant of all."*

"So does that mean I drop out of the contest and run around getting everybody's water for them?" Lily said.

"No," Dad said. "But here's what I think it does mean."

A half-hour later, the pizza, except for Joe's part, was gone, and Lily had a pretty clear idea what Dad—and Jesus—were talking about.

"You can do it, Lil," Mom said.

"Yeah," Lily said, "But I'm gonna need help."

"From some friends."

"Can I call Reni?"

"Call Kresha too," Mom said. "I think she needs a chance to make amends."

So Lily called them both, and within the hour, they were there. Mrs. Reinhold had said for Lily to get a good night's sleep, but it seemed more important to have a well-developed plan. By eleven o'clock, when Mom called for lights out, they had one.

"Please, God," Lily prayed before she drifted off. "Please let me know if this is right. From now on—whatever I do, I do it for you."

As Lily watched her Fruity Pebbles get soggy in the bowl the next morning, she couldn't decide whether she was more nervous about giving her speech or carrying out her plan with Kresha and Reni.

"What if this doesn't work, Mom?" Lily said.

"It's going to work," Mom said. "Eat your cereal."

"How can you be sure?"

"I'm not sure it's going to work for Suzy and Zooey, but I know it's going to work for you."

Kresha grinned around a bagel. "And for me?"

"You bet," Mom said, "and Reni too."

Lily considered that. She was already feeling not so jealous that Suzy had a gift and she didn't and not so angry that Suzy had resorted to scare tactics to better her odds. That was all probably a God thing. But she couldn't eat her breakfast, because she was still afraid that what was going to happen today would end the Girlz Only Group forever.

"Can we all pray before we go?" Lily asked.

"Thought you'd never ask," Mom said.

When everybody was dressed to go to the contest, including Art and Joe, they circled up in the living room and Dad led the praying. Everybody had a chance to say something if they wanted, which everyone did, even Joe, who added, "God, just don't let her freak out up there, okay? 'Cause I know I would if it was me."

"I didn't know you had a thing about speaking in front of people, Joe," Dad said later when they were on their way in the van.

"Are you kiddin' me? I'd about rather be put in front of a firing squad."

"It runs in the family," Lily said.

When they got to the high school and were making their way through the maze of halls to the Little Theatre, Dad gave Lily's hand one last squeeze. "You can do this, Lilliputian," he said. "You've got God at your back."

Lily nodded, and then she looked at Reni and Kresha. "You guys ready?" she said.

"Ready, boss!" Kresha said.

Lily let out a guffaw that felt so good she wanted to do it again. So she did.

"Okay, we gotta get serious," Reni said. "We gotta follow the plan." Kresha saluted.

"Okay, then," Lily said. "Find Suzy and tell me where she is."

Kresha and Reni disappeared into the small crowd that was gathering in the lobby. Lily stood near the coffee, juice, and donut table — where Art and Joe were busily chowing down like they hadn't just devoured half the kitchen at home — and looked around. It seemed strange to be this close to Cedar Hills Middle School — just a few blocks away — and not know everybody. But it wasn't hard to pick out the other speakers, even though they were from other middle schools. Every one of them had a white face, darting eyes, and an expression that said *please just let this be over.*

I'm with ya, Lily thought. *I feel your pain.*

She had just decided she ought to pray for all of them when Kresha came running up, socks bunched around her ankles, and hair flying in every direction except the one it was supposed to go in.

"Suzy!" she said.

"Yeah—where?" Lily said.

"Already sitting down. Fourth row. Dat side." She held up four fingers and pointed to the left.

"Okay, thanks," Lily said.

But she couldn't move. What if Suzy turned really evil on her? What if she started screaming at Lily in front of everyone? Or worse—what if she was so mad at Lily that she dropped out of Girlz Only and it broke up forever?

"Lee-lee."

Lily looked at Kresha. She was standing with her hands on her hips.

"God behind you," she said. "Now—you go, girl."

Then Kresha grinned, her eyes crinkling beneath her scraggly bangs, and Lily had to smile.

"Okay," Lily said. And straightening her shoulders, she marched into the Little Theatre.

Kresha had been pretty precise. Suzy was already sitting in the speakers' section, fourth row down and to the left. No one else was there yet, so she looked even smaller than usual, especially in the high-ceilinged theater. Lily could feel her nervousness from several rows up.

Maybe I shouldn't do this right now, Lily thought as she walked slowly down toward her. *Maybe it'll freak her out too much, and she won't be able to do her speech.*

But she'd already expressed that concern to Mom, and Mom had said, "If she reads what's on the message, how can it possibly do anything but pump her up? Remember—you're thinking like a servant now. You won't hurt her."

Lily stopped at the end of the fourth row and leaned over at the waist. "Suzy?" she said.

Suzy was so startled that she dropped her note cards on the floor.

"Let me get those for you," Lily said. She retrieved the cards from around Suzy's feet and handed them to her. They were damp and curled from Suzy's perspiring hands.

"Thank you," Suzy mumbled as she took the cards and went back to palming them.

"I just wanted to give you this," Lily said. She took out one of the two things in her pocket — an envelope — and held it out to Suzy.

Suzy blinked at it. "What is it?" she said.

"Open it and find out," Lily said.

Suzy shrank back from the envelope as if it were a boa constrictor.

"It's not anything bad, I promise," Lily said. "Open it."

First looking around as if to make sure she had an escape route, Suzy finally took the envelope and broke the seal. She pulled the paper out only halfway before she gasped, and Lily saw the look of agony cross her face. She'd already seen the letters, cut out from magazines and pasted onto the paper, just the way she'd done it herself so many times in the last few weeks.

"Don't worry," Lily said. "It's not a hate letter. Read it."

Suzy looked as if she would rather read the Bible out loud in Hebrew than take in one word that Lily — and Kresha and Reni — had glued to the paper. But she pulled it out, unfolded it with maddening slowness, and began to read the prayer they had written for her. Lily watched Suzy's eyes.

At first, they were birdlike and frightened, but as they moved down the page, they settled with relief, lit up with pleasure, and then glistened with shiny tears.

"I just wanted you to know I'm pulling for you today," Lily said.

She waited a few seconds to see if Suzy would say anything. But Mom and Dad had said that if she didn't respond right away, Lily should leave her alone to gather her thoughts.

"Yeah, she's a pretty private person," Lily had said.

Kresha had agreed, though Reni had held out for making Suzy squirm a little. But no, that wasn't being a servant, Mom and Dad kept reminding them. *Be the servant of all.*

Lily patted her pocket as she moved back up the aisle. That very verse of Scripture was printed on the other piece of paper she was carrying just so she wouldn't forget.

There were more people in the lobby when she got there, which meant things would be starting soon. She needed to talk to Zooey before then — that was the plan.

Lily stood in the middle of the crowd on her tiptoes. She craned her neck for Reni and Kresha, who were supposed to look for Zooey and report her location to Lily. But it was Joe who hobbled up behind her and whispered loudly, "She just went into the girls' bathroom. I wasn't gonna follow her in there, but she's gotta come out sooner or later."

"Thanks, Joe," Lily said.

She was feeling so emotional just then that she tried to give him a hug, but he held out a crutch and fended her off. Lily hurried off to the restroom.

There were only a few people at the sinks when Lily got there. She joined them and pretended her hands needed washing while she waited for them to leave. She could see Zooey's black ankle-high boots in one of the stalls, and she was pretty sure Zooey was connected to them.

The timing was perfect. The two ladies left at the same time, and seconds later, Zooey opened the stall door. When she saw Lily waiting for her, Zooey's gray eyes nearly popped from her head.

You'll have the element of surprise on your side, Mom had told Lily. *Take advantage of it quickly.*

"Hi," Lily said. "I need to talk to you before they start."

"Suzy," Zooey said. "I have to go find Suzy. She needs me."

She was sounding as if she'd been programmed like a computer. Even when Lily put her hand on her arm to keep her from leaving, it felt stiff as a piece of metal.

"Suzy's fine," Lily said. "I just saw her."

Zooey looked at the door, her eyes frantic. Lily put a hand on her shoulder.

"Don't worry, Zooey," Lily said. "I didn't yell at her, and I'm not gonna yell at you. I just wanna say that the way you and Suzy have treated me has really hurt me, but I think I understand why you did it, and I forgive you." Lily let go of her shoulder. "That's all I wanted to say."

Give her a chance to respond if she wants to, Mom had advised Lily, *but if she doesn't, leave her alone so she can process on her own. This is supposed to make her feel better in the long run, not worse.*

Zooey didn't look like she was going to say anything—maybe for the rest of her life. So Lily said, "I have to go—they're gonna start soon," and left the restroom.

"Lilianna—there you are," Mrs. Reinhold said. She was hurrying toward her across the now almost vacant lobby. "Go backstage and join the others. They're all gathered back there to hear the order of presentation and get themselves together."

"Okay," was all Lily could say. As she followed the signs to the backstage area, she felt wilted, and the day had barely started. But it seemed like the important part of the day was over. After what she'd just done, the speech almost didn't matter.

Still, when she reached the group of seven other speakers in an area behind the side curtains and heard a bald-headed man already reading off the order list, the fear surged up again.

"First up—" he said. "—Lilianna Robbins. Is she here?"

Lily raised her hand.

"Okay, get ready," Mr. Baldhead said. "As soon as they finish with the formalities, you're on. If you need water, it's right over there."

He pointed to a table, but Lily didn't go to it. She knew if she put one single thing in her mouth, she'd throw up right on stage. As she closed her eyes and went through her lines one more time, she wasn't sure that wouldn't happen anyway. Her stomach was churning what little breakfast she'd eaten, and the hair on the back of her neck was getting damper by the minute.

I don't like this, she thought. *Why am I even doing it? I wish we'd have a tornado or something so they'd cancel it.*

Lily sighed and rubbed her palms against the sides of her skirt to dry them off. Mom and Dad were right—she sure didn't do this for the joy of it.

"Our first contestant comes to us from neighboring Cedar Hills Middle School," some man on stage was saying.

Some people in the crowd cheered. Lily was pretty sure it was Art and Joe and Kresha and Reni. Kresha didn't whistle, though. Dad had told her last night that she really ought to save those great whistles for sporting events. She had then spent half an hour teaching Joe how to do it.

"So, without further delay," the man said, "I give you Lilianna Robbins."

There was more clapping and cheering, but Lily barely heard it. Somehow she got out onto the stage and found the podium. Somehow she looked out at the audience and smiled. And somehow she got out her first line and her second and her third until she heard herself winding up. When she gave her last line and paused, looking at the audience, she saw Mrs. Reinhold clapping for all she was worth and looking proud. She saw Reni and Art and Kresha standing up and Joe waving a crutch from his seat. And she saw Mom and Dad, exchanging those mushy-eyed glances and beaming up at her.

I did my best, Lily thought as, weak-kneed, she walked offstage. *And thank you, God—that it's over.*

"Nice job," Mr. Baldhead whispered to her. "Where's Number Two—"

He went off in search of the next green-in-the-gills person, and Lily sagged against the water table. As soon as he got the second person going on stage, he hurried back.

"Anybody seen Number Six?" he whispered. He consulted his clipboard. "Suzanne Wheeler?"

"I know she's here," Lily said. "I saw her earlier."

"Check the bathroom for me, would you, Number One?" he said.

"Me?" Lily said.

"You know her, don't you?"

"Yeah," Lily said. "Okay."

"She still has some time, but I like to have all my ducks in a row," he said.

Lily fumbled her way through props and pieces of scenery and found the girls' restroom next to the paint cabinet. It didn't look as if anybody was in there when she first opened the door. But when she whispered, "Suzy?" she heard a soft moan.

"Suzy—is that you?" Lily said.

She bent over and looked under the door to one of the two stalls. She saw not only Suzy's feet but her legs and part of her lap. She was on her knees, facing the toilet.

"Suzy—are you puking?" Lily said.

"Yeah," was the weak reply.

"Do you need any help?" Lily said. "I mean, not with puking—but I mean, with not puking—or something?"

There was another moan and then the flushing of the toilet. Suzy got up and the stall door came open. She leaned against the doorway.

"I'm done," she said.

She stumbled toward the sinks, and Lily grabbed her before she plowed right into one. There was a chair over to the side, and Lily led Suzy to it.

"Sit down," she said. "I'll get you a cold cloth for your forehead."

"Don't get my hair wet," Suzy said. "Zooey'll have a fit."

Lily wet a paper towel, folded it carefully, and put it on Suzy's forehead while Suzy held back her bangs.

"Don't get any on my outfit either," she said. "Zooey helped me pick it out."

"Don't worry about it—you look great."

"I don't feel great. I'm so scared."

"Everybody's scared," Lily said.

Suzy opened her eyes. "Do you see anybody else in there throwing up?" she said. She closed her eyes again and sighed. "I hate this part. I want to get up there so bad, but there's part of me that wants to run and hide."

"And throw up," Lily said.

"Yeah. Maybe I wasn't cut out for this, you know?"

"Are you kidding?" Lily said. "You have a *gift* for speaking. Even my mom and dad say so."

"Nuh-uh," Suzy said.

"Yuh-huh. You're gonna be amazing."

"I hope the judges think so."

"They will."

They were quiet for a few minutes, and Lily noticed that her heart wasn't hammering so hard inside her chest anymore. She no longer felt like joining Suzy at the toilet.

Is that because it's finally over? Lily thought. *Or because Suzy's letting me put a cold rag on her head?*

Whatever it was, Lily silently thanked God for Suzy, which gave her an idea—a servant idea.

"You want me to pray with you?" Lily said.

Suzy nodded.

Lily took both of her hands, then bowed her head, closed her eyes, and prayed—for Suzy to be able to calm down and do her best—for the judges to see her gift—for Suzy to feel good about herself.

She was about to say, "Amen," when Suzy said, "Don't forget to ask him to make us all friends again."

Lily did—with a lump in her throat. It was probably going to happen with Suzy—but she still wasn't so sure about Zooey.

"I think you're ready," Lily said. "Unless you wanna throw up some more."

"No—I'm okay." Suzy stood up, but she didn't look Lily in the eye. "Thanks," she said to the bathroom floor. "And—Lily—I'm sorry about that stuff I did to you. And, Lily, it wasn't Zooey." By now her voice was so low, Lily could barely hear her. "It was all me."

"Oh," Lily said.

She waited for the anger to well up and turn her face blotchy, but that didn't happen. Instead, she said to Suzy, "I hate it that you did that, but I forgive you."

Suzy didn't seem to be able to say anything. She just flung herself at Lily and hugged her neck.

"I think it's gonna be okay," Lily said over Suzy's shoulder. "Everything's gonna be okay." Then she held Suzy out at arm's length. "Except your outfit. We better not get it wrinkled, or Zooey'll have a cow."

"A whole herd," Suzy said. She sucked in air. "I'm really nervous, Lily."

"Yeah—but that'll disappear the minute you start talking."

"How do you know?"

"Because it always does with you. I think that's a God thing."

By the time they returned to backstage, Mr. Baldhead was looking a little distressed. He seemed relieved to see Suzy and wouldn't let her out of his reach until it was finally her turn. Lily gave her one last hug before she went on, and then she stood in the wings and watched her, just out of sight of the audience. Mr. Baldhead hadn't let anybody else do that, but he seemed to sense that it was important.

When Suzy stepped up to the podium, there was a sound from the audience, almost an "ah" like when somebody brings a baby on *Oprah*. They obviously thought little Suzy was adorable.

Yeah, but wait'll they hear her speak, Lily thought.

"A person without a purpose in life," Suzy began.

Her voice was pure and strong and warm, just like she was pulling them all into a conversation. Lily couldn't help grinning as she heard and watched Suzy perform her speaking magic.

Once again, when Suzy was finished, the audience went nuts. Even Mr. Baldhead was clapping — so hard that he almost forgot to get Number Seven ready to go on.

When Suzy came through the side curtains, she was glowing. Not the I'm-so-glad-that-is-over kind of glow, Lily thought, but an I-love-this-stuff glow.

"You were awesome," Lily whispered.

"Was I? No — I wasn't — was I?"

Lily nodded. "You were."

They stood there, side by side but not talking, until Mr. Baldhead told all the speakers, "The judges are ready to announce the winner."

Lily's heart was pounding again, and she knew Suzy's must be too.

"Because of the importance of the state contest," the announcer was saying, "the judges have selected an alternate who will also prepare for the competition and be ready to step in should circumstances not permit our winner to appear at the state contest. We have the utmost confidence in both of our selections today."

Lily held her breath. An alternate? That meant there was still a chance she could be a winner.

"Our first runner-up, who will act as an alternate," the announcer said, "is Jason Hobarth."

The crowd cheered from far away. *It isn't me,* Lily thought as a skinny seventh-grade boy brushed past her on his way to the stage. *I didn't win.*

"And our winner," the announcer said, "who will represent us at the New Jersey Seventh Grade State Speech Contest, is —"

"Come on!" Lily whispered.

"Suzanne Wheeler!"

There was a shriek from the audience — it had to be Zooey — followed by a roar that said the crowd approved. Next to her, Suzy began to shake.

"Are you crying?" Lily said.

"Uh-huh," Suzy said.

"But you won," Lily said.

"I know." Suzy looked up at Lily with tear-sparkly eyes. "And I wanted to more than anything. I love doing this."

Lily knew it was true. It wasn't relief she saw in Suzy — it was pure joy. It didn't matter how much she was going to have to worry or fret or throw up between now and the state contest, Suzy loved what she was doing.

"Wow," Lily said as Suzy made her way out onto the stage. "Just — wow."

Chapter 11

The minute Suzy was off the stage, trophy in hand, Mr. Baldhead whisked her away. A photographer from the *Burlington County Times* wanted to get a picture of her for the newspaper.

A pang of jealousy went through Lily, and it didn't stop as she watched Suzy pose for her picture and answer a reporter's questions. It didn't stop as she watched Mrs. Reinhold hug Suzy in the lobby and go on for five minutes to Suzy's parents about what an exceptional speaker she was. And — the worst part — it didn't stop as she witnessed Zooey presenting Suzy with a bouquet of carnations. Lily felt her face going blotchy, and she was certain the blotches were envy green.

Mom was suddenly beside Lily, arm around her shoulders.

"How you holding up, Lil?" she said.

"Not so good," Lily said. "I still wish it was me — I know that's bad."

"It's human," Mom said. "Look at all the attention Suzy's getting. That has to feel good to her, so why wouldn't you want to be feeling that right now?"

"It would be better than what I *am* feeling," Lily said. "I'm so jealous."

"Like I said, that's human," Mom said. "But you don't want to let it go on."

"What do I do?" Lily said.

"Be the servant of all," Mom said.

Lily looked at Suzy, whose smile was so big it nearly met in the back of her head. She had every reason to be happy.

"Right now?" Lily said.

"Right now," Mom said.

Lily took a deep breath and went over to Suzy, who was standing in the middle of an admiring knot of people—Mrs. Reinhold, Mr. and Mrs. Wheeler, Suzy's two sisters, Zooey, Zooey's mother, and the county speech coordinator, who had been making all the announcements on stage.

Is there anybody else who wants to come over here and watch me crawl? Lily thought.

But she waited for the man to stop talking, and then she said, "Excuse me? I just wanted to congratulate Suzy."

A silence fell over the group, as if nobody was quite sure how this was going to turn out. All except Suzy, who held out her arms for Lily to hug her.

"You deserved to win," Lily said. "You were the best."

"Now—weren't you in the contest too?" said the county coordinator.

Lily pulled away from Suzy. He was talking to her.

"Yes, sir," Lily said. *And I must have been incredible if you even have to ask that!*

"Huh," he said. "Well, it's very nice of you to come over here and congratulate the competition. That shows real character. What's your name?"

"Lily Robbins," Lily said.

"And she is definitely a character," Mrs. Reinhold said. She smiled at Lily—a rare thing—and reached out to squeeze her hand. It made Lily feel a whole lot better.

It also helped that the whole family and Reni and Kresha went to Friendly's for an ice-cream lunch. Lily was starving and had a chocolate milk shake *and* a banana split.

"You're going to split if you eat all that," Dad said.

"It's okay," Mom said. "It'll make up for the all the meals she hasn't eaten in the last two weeks. Are we done with this I-can't-possibly-eat thing, Lil? I was starting to get concerned."

"Wasn't I eating?" Lily said.

"No," Art said, "you were stressing."

"Well, forget that," Lily said. "Ren, are you gonna eat your cherry, or can I have it?"

Everything seemed to be falling into place. Lily could tell because she did want to eat, and she went right to sleep that night, almost in mid-prayer. *And* she could think about other things besides giving a speech. But there was still that place in her that hurt—that place that belonged to Zooey.

"What are we gonna do if she doesn't want to be in Girlz Only anymore?" Lily said to Reni at Sunday school the next morning.

"That'd be a bummer," Reni said. "I liked meeting in her basement."

"It's not just that," Lily said. "If you and me and Kresha and Suzy want to get the group back together and she doesn't, then are we gonna be able to do it anyway? What if Suzy feels like she has to be loyal to Zooey and Kresha keeps running back and forth?"

"Looks that way," Reni said. She nodded toward the other side of the Sunday school room, where Kresha was just arriving and hugging Zooey and Suzy as if she hadn't seen them for weeks. It didn't seem that anything had changed, in spite of Lily's attempts to be their servant.

"Now that's somethin'," Reni said. "You bring Kresha to church the first time, and now she hangs out with Zooey and Suzy when she's here."

Lily started to nod, but she stopped. Zooey was crossing the room, headed straight for Lily.

"What does *she* want?" Reni said. "Lily, if she starts rubbing it in your face that you lost to Suzy, so help me—"

But Zooey didn't look like she was going to rub anything anywhere. She looked like she was going to cry.

Be the servant of all, said the piece of paper tucked into Lily's pocket.

She took a step toward Zooey. "Are you okay, Zo?" she said. "Are you crying?"

If she hadn't been before, she was now. Zooey's face crumpled, and tears poured down her face.

"Yikes," Lily said. "What's wrong? Do you want to go in the bathroom with me?"

Zooey shook her head, wisps of hair sticking to the wet on her cheeks.

"I'm so sorry, Lily," she said. "I was so hateful to you, and I'm really sorry."

It struck Lily that if someone had come into the room just then and announced that a mistake had been made and Lily was the speech alternate, instead of that Jason kid, she couldn't have been as happy as she was at this moment.

"It was pretty awful," Lily said to her, "but it's over now. We all messed up, and we can all fix it."

"You want to?" Zooey bleated, like a pitiful little sheep. "You aren't just gonna hate me for the rest of my life?"

"How could I hate you?" Lily said. "You're my friend."

"Oh, Lily!" Zooey said.

She fell against Lily and sobbed. By now the entire Sunday school class was focused on the scene, amid some snickering, and it was pretty embarrassing. Lily looked to Reni for help.

"Come on, Zooey," Reni said. "You and me'll go to the bathroom and get you calmed down. You're freaking out."

Zooey let Reni take her by the arm, but she cowered as they walked.

"Are you gonna do something to me, Reni?" Lily heard Zooey say. "I know I deserve it, but please don't hurt me."

"You're such a goofball, Zooey," Reni said. "Of course I'm not gonna hurt ya—"

As Lily watched them go, she felt warmth nearby. She looked to see Kresha on one side of her and Suzy on the other.

"Can we sit with you guys?" Suzy said.

"On one condition," Lily said.

Panic crossed Suzy's face.

"That we Girlz always talk everything out from now on and never take sides again."

"Cross my heart and hope to die," Suzy said.

"Cross my heart too," Kresha said. Then she frowned. "But I have to die?" she said.

There was plenty of time to explain that to her, because the Girlz could barely stand to be separated for the rest of the day. All of them, even Reni, were at the bench before school on Monday.

"Don't you have orchestra practice?" Suzy said.

"No—I usually just practice on my own before school," Reni said. "But I was telling my mom about everything that's happened, you know, with us, and she said she thinks I need to balance myself out more and not practice quite so much."

"Then you can help us get Suzy ready for the state contest," Zooey said. "Now, I'm thinking she should wear a darker color this time, to make her look more serious—"

Reni and Lily rolled their eyes at each other, but the eyes they rolled were happy.

Over the next few weeks, the Girlz Only Group began to meet again in Zooey's basement three days a week to giggle and talk and pray and prep Suzy for her big-deal event. Lily still had the occasional pang of jealousy, but when she tried to put herself in Suzy's place, she got nauseous. God, she decided, had strange ways of reminding you of what you were — and weren't — supposed to do.

It was so good to be back with her Girlz that Lily didn't think much about the whole winning thing until one morning a few weeks after the county contest, when Mrs. Reinhold took her out into the hall during class.

"Busted," Ashley whispered as she left.

Lily ignored her. Ashley and her crowd *so* didn't bother her that much anymore.

"Lilianna," Mrs. Reinhold said when they were outside the door, "the county speech contest coordinator called me yesterday. Do you remember him?"

"Yes," Lily said. She also remembered that he hadn't remembered her ten minutes after the contest was over.

"He wanted to talk to me about you," Mrs. Reinhold said.

"Me?" Lily said.

"He told me that the county commission is starting a program on character and as part of that, they are offering a prize to the student at each grade level in each school who shows the most traits of good character." Mrs. Reinhold smiled at Lily. "He suggested I nominate you."

"Me?" Lily said again.

"He was very impressed that you came up to Suzanne to congratulate her after she'd taken the prize and you hadn't. When I told him more about you, he was more convinced than ever that you should be the candidate from Cedar Hills Middle, seventh grade. I told him I thought it would be more fair if we opened this up to all the teachers to make nominations and vote, perhaps with a panel for the finalists where we could ask you questions—"

"Excuse me, Mrs. Reinhold," Lily said. "But is this a competition?"

"Well, yes, of sorts, I suppose," Mrs. Reinhold said.

"Then I don't think so," Lily said. "But thank you for offering."

Mrs. Reinhold looked at her closely. "Competition is not a bad thing, Lilianna. It certainly improved your speaking skills."

"I know," Lily said, "but I think I've had enough for a while. I think I need to focus on helping Suzy get ready, and I'm helping my little brother with his physical therapy so he can get back into sports. Besides, our whole family is gonna be going to a bunch of different colleges in the spring so my older brother can audition for music schools. We're all gonna go and support him."

"Now you see why they want you in the character contest," Mrs. Reinhold said. "But, Lilianna, don't neglect the development of your gifts while you're helping everyone else."

"Wow," Lily said. Something had just struck her, and it was dazzling.

"Wow?" Mrs. Reinhold said. "Define that term for me."

"Well, I was just thinking, Wow—maybe helping people develop their gifts *is* my gift. I mean, wow, that's something."

"Lilianna, my dear," Mrs. Reinhold said, "I think it is *you* who are something."

A lot more wow thoughts came to Lily over the next couple of days.

When she and the Girlz were making Valentines in Zooey's basement, she thought, *Love is more important than winning.*

When Zooey and Kresha volunteered to be in the church Easter production they were already starting to rehearse for, she thought, *Getting them to notice God is the best thing any of us Girlz ever did.*

When Shad Shifferdecker came to her locker one day before school and said, "Is that Zooey chick still leavin' you weird notes?" she had to think twice.

"It wasn't Zooey — it was Suzy," Lily said.

"Ain't Zooey the one that used to be fat only now she's all thin?"

"Yeah," Lily said.

"It was her — I saw her about six times stuffin' paper into your locker. I was on stake-out."

Lily didn't bother to ask why. She was too stunned thinking about Suzy taking all the blame, and she thought, *So other people were being the servant of all besides me.*

She looked at Shad and said, "How come you're so into all this anyway? You used to hate my guts."

"I'm over that," he said and strutted away.

Wow, Lily thought, *there are some things you just never understand.*

And when all the Girlz went to the state speech contest and watched Suzy take first runner-up, she thought, *When you find out what God wants you to do, you're always gonna win somehow.* Sitting in that big auditorium, watching her tiny friend astound everybody with her speech, Lily felt more like a winner than she ever had.

She needed all those good thoughts and feelings around at the end of February, when Mom and Dad called a family meeting. By now, Joe was off of his crutches, but he didn't bounce around the room that day, cast and all, the way he usually did. From the way Mom and Dad were acting, this was some pretty serious stuff.

"All right, dish, you guys," Art said when they were all sitting down. "You're driving us nuts with the suspense."

"Is this about that kid we're adopting?" Joe said. "When's she comin', anyway?"

"This spring," Dad said, "And it's not about that —"

"Did something fall through with the new addition?" Art said. He glanced at the large piece of plastic that shielded them from the dust of construction. "They do seem to be takin' their time."

"No—the addition will be finished within two weeks," Dad said. "Or so they've promised."

"Then what's up?" Joe said. "You're killin' me here."

Mom looked at Dad, who looked at his hands for what seemed like forever. Finally, he said, "I have an opportunity—well, *we* have an opportunity, as a family—that I'm not sure we can pass up. But it's going to mean a lot of change for all of us, and maybe some sacrifices."

"We're getting twins," Joe said.

"Shut up, man," Art said. He looked hard at Dad. "So—what's this opportunity?"

"I've been invited to be a visiting Fellow at Magdalene College, Oxford University."

"Where's that?" Joe said.

"England," Lily said. She hadn't been coloring in all those geography maps for nothing.

"For how long?" Art said.

"For a year," Dad said, "beginning this August."

"And we're all going?" Lily said.

"If we can determine that this is something God wants us all to do," Dad said.

"He doesn't want me to do it, I can tell you that right now," Art said. "That's my senior year, man. I don't want to miss that! What about my scholarships and stuff? What if I have auditions at, like, Julliard in the fall or somethin'?"

"That can be worked out," Mom said. "One of us will fly back here with you for those."

"Yeah, but, dude, I'll be a nobody at school—my senior year!"

"You could do your senior year by correspondence," Dad said. "Your mother would be homeschooling Lily and Joe and our new girl, so she could tutor you as well."

"Homeschool?" Lily said. "Just us?"

"Yeah, but what about sports?" Joe said.

"Honey, you have never *seen* soccer like they have in England," Mom said. "You'll come back here and out dribble everybody."

"Oh," Joe said. "That might not be so bad."

Art grunted.

"You'll be able to travel while we're there," Dad said. "Have experiences you could never dream of having here."

"I've already dreamed up the experiences I want, and they're *all* right here," Art said.

"There are other options for you, Art," Dad said.

"Like what?" Art said.

"We'll talk about those with you individually later," Dad said. "Now, Joe, it sounds like you're in favor of it."

"Yeah—if I get to play soccer—and baseball."

"Cricket," Mom said.

"Huh?"

"It's called cricket over there."

"What about you, Lilliputian?" Dad said.

Lily hadn't realized it until now, but there was a big lump in her throat. And tears were gathering behind her eyes.

"I don't know," she said. "Me and the Girlz—we just got back together. I don't think I want to leave them for a whole year."

"That would be hard for you," Mom said. "We realize that, and that's why we're asking for your input."

"Then I vote no," Art said. He set his jaw and crossed his arms. Lily hadn't seen him do that since he was about thirteen. She decided not to take that route herself. She had a better idea.

113

"Can I have time to pray about it?" Lily said.

"Of course," Dad said. "We all need to pray on our own—we need to pray together as a family—we need to have our friends pray for us. We have to know that this is something God wants us to do."

Everyone agreed, and the meeting broke up. Lily was in her room for only a minute when Art knocked on the door.

"We have to talk," he said.

Lily pointed to a vacant place on the bed. But Otto growled when Art tried to sit down, so he perched himself on the edge of Lily's desk.

"Look," he said, "this year in England thing is totally gonna ruin life as I know it—and I can see you're leanin' that way too. You got your own thing going here now, and you don't want to leave it, right?"

"Yeah," Lily said slowly.

"If you and I work together, we can probably swing Joe over to our side. All he cares about is sports, so if we can get him healed and on some select soccer team here or something, he won't want to leave either." Art held out his hands, palms up. "When it comes to a vote, that's three to two. We win—and we stay here."

"It seems like Dad really wants to do this, though," Lily said.

"So let him go—or at least wait 'til we're out of school so our lives aren't all messed up by what he wants to do. I mean, we're a family. So what do you say—are you on my side?"

"I don't think we should take sides," Lily said. "I just got through doing that, and it didn't work out."

"So you'd sacrifice everything for Dad and go without even putting up a fight," Art said. His eyes were narrowed into slits.

"I don't know," Lily said. "I have to pray about it—and talk to the Girlz. But I know taking sides and trying to make something happen isn't what we should do. Like Dad said—"

"Yeah, I heard the whole God thing," Art said.

"But I thought you did your music *for* God," Lily said. "That's what you told me."

"Yeah, well, God's here in Burlington, New Jersey, for me," Art said.

"He could be in England too," Lily said.

Art glared at her. "Traitor."

"Am not."

"I can see I'm gonna have to fight this on my own," Art said, standing up.

"I'll pray for you too," Lily said.

"You're gettin' to be, like, the totally spiritual one in the family," Art said. And then he left.

Lily lay on her bed next to a snoozing Otto for a long time after that, thinking about what Art said.

"God, is that true?" she said to her empty room. "Am I getting to be spiritual? Am I, like, getting in touch with you?"

It was a good thought, one that made her heart stop pounding, dried her palms, made her feel hungry.

It chased away the vision of spending even a day apart from her Girlz and replaced it with Lily reaching up for a prize—the next prize in her life—whatever that was going to be.

"You know what, Otto?" she said.

He gave her a grunt.

"I think as long as I do what I think God wants me to do, I'm always gonna win. Ya think?"

If he agreed, he didn't say. But Lily went to sleep knowing God agreed. And that was all she needed.

the **Lily** series

Horse Crazy Lily

Nancy Rue

Chapter 1

"Hey, Lily—you comin' or what?"

Lily Robbins glared into the mirror she was standing in front of. She was looking at her own redheaded self, but the glare was intended for her seventeen-year-old brother, Art. He was two floors down and probably tossing his keys from one hand to the other.

"Like he has so much to do on a Saturday afternoon," Lily said to the mirror.

But he *had* agreed to drive her out to Suzy's birthday party.

With a sigh, she untangled her way-long-for-a-twelve-year-old legs and got to the door, where she poked her curly head out and yelled back, "Don't have a cow! I'll be right down."

"Define 'right down,'" Art yelled back.

"Two minutes."

"I'm pulling out of the driveway in exactly two minutes."

Lily scrambled to the closet and dragged out the boots she'd cleaned up for Suzy's party. They brought on a grin. What a great idea Suzy had come up with for her birthday—an afternoon of horseback riding for her and all the Girlz—Lily, Zooey, Reni, and

117

Kresha. Lily had never been on a horse, though she'd always thought it sounded way cool. She felt like this was as much a present for her as for Suzy.

Lily glanced at her watch and then whipped her mane of curls around, looking for the gift she'd taken a half hour to wrap. She had put it right on the bed — and it should be easy to spot.

Since she'd moved into her new room up here in the attic a week ago, she hadn't had a chance to decorate — what her mother referred to as "cluttering up the place." The only things currently cluttering it were her stuffed animals. She could barely function without them, especially the giant panda, China, who she leaned against during her talking-to-God time every night — with Otto by her side, of course.

"Otto!" Lily said.

She heard him grunt from under the bed, and she dove for it.

"Tell me you don't have Suzy's present!" she said as she lifted up the dust ruffle.

Otto, her little gray mutt, blinked at her through the darkness.

"You do — you are *so* evil!"

Lily made a snatch for the blue-covered package and managed to get hold of the ribbon. While Otto tugged one way, she yanked the other and pulled dog and gift out into daylight. Otto's scruffy top hair stood up on end.

"I'm lee-ving —" Art called from below.

"Don't! I'm coming!" Lily cried. Grabbing onto the gift — and dangling Otto in midair in the process — she grabbed her denim jacket with her free hand and tore down both flights of stairs. Otto growled and snarled the whole way, but he didn't loosen his little jaws of steel, in spite of Lily's steady stream of "Drop it, you little demon seed! I spent my whole last week's allowance on that!"

Art, arms folded, was waiting at the bottom of the stairs.

"Grab him, Art," Lily said. "Make him let go."

"You gotta be kidding," Art said. He took a step backward. "I'm not touching that dog. He'll bite my hand off."

"What in the world—" Mom said. She appeared out of the dining room, dust rag in one hand, can of furniture polish in the other. Her mouth twitched—in that way it did instead of going into a whole smile. "Otto," she said in her crisp coach's voice. "Drop it."

Otto, of course, didn't—at least not until Mom sprayed some polish into the air above her head. Otto let go of the present and, tucking his tail between his scrawny legs, disappeared up the stairs. He didn't like spray cans.

"Can we *go* now?" Art said.

"Have fun," Mom said. "And, Lil—don't make any plans to spend the night with anybody tonight. You know tomorrow is a big day."

Lily nodded as she ran toward Art's Subaru—nicknamed Ruby Sue. She managed to slide in before Art got it into gear.

"It's that place over in Columbus, right?" Art said.

"Uh-huh."

"Could she have picked a place farther away?"

"It's the only riding stables in South Jersey, I think," Lily said.

"Tha-at's an exaggeration." Art had picked up a new habit of dragging out his words in a bored voice. Lily thought it must be some cool thing musicians did.

"So—what do you think this Tessa chick is going to be like?" he said with a snicker. "Her mother must have really had it in for her to give her a name like Tessa. What's thaaat about?"

Lily rolled her eyes in his direction. "Her mother probably *did* have it in for her, or she wouldn't have been in all those foster homes.

119

And we're not supposed to talk about all the stuff that's happened to her unless she brings it up, remember?"

"Like I'm going to forget. We heard it about a dozen times."

Lily had to agree—he was right about that. Ever since Mom and Dad had found out that the adoption agency had a child for them, they'd been holding family meetings to talk about Tessa, who was about to become their nine-year-old sister.

"She's had a rough time," Dad had explained. "She hasn't had any of the things you kids have had, including love or security or a family."

Mom was a little more direct: "You can't be doing your brother-and-sister routine while she's getting adjusted. No teasing—no kicking under the table—am I clear?"

"Have you noticed how different they are lately when they talk about her?" Art said now. "Now that they've actually met her?"

"No," Lily said. "Well—I did notice that Mom's cleaning the entire house with a toothbrush to get ready for her. You think Tessa's a neat freak?"

Art shook his head. "I saw a list of child psychologists on Dad's desk."

"Don't they send, like, mental patients to them?"

"Nah—half the kids I know are in therapy," Art said. "Whatever the chick's got going on, it's probably not that big a deal. I think Mom and Dad are freakin' a little."

The rest of the way to the stables, Lily forgot about horses and thought about Tessa. The Robbinses had known for a while that they were going to adopt a child, and Lily had been all over it—another girl to help her survive two brothers. She'd gotten excited about fixing up her old room for Tessa, but Mom had said they should just paint it white and let her decorate it how she wanted to, since she'd never had her own room before.

When Mom and Dad had come back from meeting her, Lily had gone to Mom with a list of possible sister activities they could do together. Mom had twisted her mouth a little and then said, "I know how you are, Lil—everything 950 percent—but, hon, you can't take Tessa on as your latest thing. Don't start reading child psychology books—"

"Mom, I'm so over trying to find my thing—"

"Good—then let's just let her get settled in and get to know her."

So Lily had been forced to put the whole thing in the back of her mind, behind math homework and Shakespeare Club and, of course, Girlz Only Group. She'd prayed for Tessa every night, but that was about all. Until now.

What if she's in a gang or something? she thought. *Is she gonna get off the plane tomorrow with a tattoo?*

"So is this it?" Art said. "Double H Stables." He snickered again. "Now thaaat's original."

"Herbert Hajek, Owner," Lily read from the plank that hung under the Double H logo on the gate that Art had pulled up to. "Of *course* it's going to be Double H. What else would they call it?"

Art raised an eyebrow in the direction of the tiny stables tucked between two maple trees. "Don't get your hopes up, Lil," he said. "I don't think this guy raises thoroughbreds."

"Reni's mom's bringing me home," Lily said as she climbed out of Ruby Sue. Which was good, because she'd had about enough of Art making everything sound worse than it was.

She forgot about Art—and Tessa—the minute Zooey, Kresha, Suzy, and Reni burst out of the stables, all wearing jeans and boots and bandanas tied to various places.

"This is going to be the *best!*" Zooey said as she tugged at Lily's arm. "We each get to ride our own horse and—"

"I get the wery strong horse!" Kresha said. Lily knew she was excited because her Croatian accent was slipping in. W's replaced v's when that happened.

Reni grabbed Lily's hand—the one Zooey *wasn't* wringing out like a dishrag—and tugged her toward the stables. She didn't have to say anything. Best friends, Lily had discovered, could communicate without words. Reni's chocolate-brown eyes, dancing in the glow of her matching-brown face, said that for once Zooey wasn't exaggerating. It was going to be awesome.

Lily let them usher her into the stables. "Awesome" didn't even begin to describe what she saw when they finally let go of her and let her look around.

It was dim inside, but even in the half-light she could tell the wooden floors were swept clean. The sun that crept in from the open doors on the other end brought eight stalls into view, four on either side of the wide hallway, each with the top half of its door open.

I bet that's where you prop yourself up to give the horses apples and sugar cubes and stuff, Lily thought. The smell was a mixture of hay and leather and—okay, maybe the *faint* odor of horse poop. But nothing had ever smelled as good.

"You girlies ready to ride?" said a voice from the open doorway.

Lily could make out only a silhouette as the Girlz all ran out to him. What she found in the sunlight was a man not much taller than her own five-foot-five—tall for a seventh grader but not for a man who had shoulders that looked like a set of football pads. She decided he'd be a lot taller if he weren't quite so bow-legged.

"I'll take that as a yes," the man said as the Girlz swarmed around him. He was wearing a blue bandana, tied tightly around his head so that he slightly resembled a cue ball with bright eyes. Lily didn't have a chance to see what color they were before he planted a battered hat onto his head and pulled the brim down almost to his nose.

"This is Herbie," Zooey said, giggling like a piccolo.

Herbie nodded at Lily and then at the line of horses that waited patiently along the wide dirt path the Girlz were standing on.

"First thing, Georgie and I will get you girlies up in those saddles," he said. His voice was as clipped and snappy as any other South Jersey accent Lily had ever heard. *That's funny,* she thought. *I expected him to talk like he was from Texas or something.*

That didn't make the idea of climbing up into one of those saddles any less exciting — or any less scary.

As Herbie showed Suzy how to put one foot in the stirrup and hoist herself up so she could swing the other leg over the saddle, Reni pointed to a horse the color of a brownie with a crooked white marking on his face that was shaped just like milk pouring out of a pitcher.

"This one's Big Jake," Reni said. "He's yours." Her voice took on a hint of envy. "I think he's the biggest one of all."

Lily agreed, but she couldn't nod her head. She'd never been this close to a horse before, and she'd never known they were quite this big. She had to look up to see under his neck, which he was now tossing around like he was impatient to get this party started.

Lily stood staring at him while the rest of the Girlz swung up into their saddles. Her mouth was starting to go dry.

Maybe this wasn't such a good idea, she thought, trying to lick her lips. *This is a big animal. I don't know what to do with something like this — yikes!*

"Your turn, girlie," Herbie said. He nodded at the stirrup. "Put your left foot right in there."

Lily felt a long pang of fear go through her—but she managed to stick her right foot into the stirrup. Herbie shook his head.

"Oh, sorry!" Lily said. "I always get right and left mixed up—" Actually, she never did, but right now her thoughts were like a herd of terrified ants.

When she finally fumbled her way into the saddle, her long right leg flailing the air for one endless, embarrassing moment before her foot found the other stirrup, Herbie said, "All right, girlies. We're all going to be together so I'll be watching your horses, but there are a few things you need to know."

Yeah, Lily thought. *Like how to get down!* She leaned over to look at the ground. The height was dizzying.

What if I fall? Lily thought. *I could break a leg! Or my neck!*

"That's all you need to know, " Herbie said. He started off toward the one empty-saddled horse on the path and then stopped. "Oh, one more thing—if you have any trouble with your horse, just say—in a calm voice, now—'I have a situation.' " He tipped his head back to look up at them. "You girlies ready to ride?"

He was answered with an assortment of yeses and giggles. But Lily didn't join in. She wanted to shout right now—"I have a situation! I don't want to go!"

But Big Jake threw his head back and shook his stringy mane and blew air out of his nostrils. *He* obviously *did.*

No sooner had the line of horses begun to move—one steed's nose buried in the tail of the one in front of it—than Big Jake tossed his head once more. And then he took off—ahead of the others—with Lily hanging on.

She screamed for all she was worth, "I have a situation!"

the **Lily** series

The **Values** & **Virtues** Book

Nancy Rue

zonder**kidz**

I'm Supposed to Have Integrity?

**The man of integrity walks securely,
but he who takes crooked paths will be found out.**
Proverbs 10:9

Zooey sometimes feels like school is a complete waste of time. She's in what she calls the "dumb classes," and even *those* are hard for her, so she feels like an idiot for six hours every day. As if that weren't bad enough, she usually has what feels like ten tons of homework, so she gets to feel idiotic at *home* too! Zooey's solution? Pretend you don't care what grades you make. Blow off your teachers. And forget even trying to do schoolwork at home.

Suzy is really gifted at sports. She can kick tail in gymnastics, soccer, softball, *and* volleyball, and she hopes she gets a growth spurt soon so she can compete in girls' basketball too. Quiet and considerate as she is, Suzy hates to lose in any sports competition, and she'll do just about anything to win. When it looks like doing her best isn't going to be enough, she isn't willing to give up. Suzy's solution? Get away with as much stretching of the rules and dirty playing as you can, intimidate your opponents, and if you lose, sulk for days and blame it on everybody else, including your own teammates.

Reni is a natural leader, and nowhere is that more evident than in orchestra. After all, she *is* first chair violin and an All-State representative. Other kids in the orchestra tend to look up to her and see her as their spokesperson, and most of the time, Reni rises to the occasion. Sometimes, however, she rises just a little too high, becoming critical, snapping at people when they're doing stuff she considers "lame" and getting jealous when someone *else* tries to rise. Reni's solution? Remind other people just how superior she is and just how lucky they are to have her in charge. When that doesn't work, she gathers the supporters she does have and declares war.

Lily is a doer, and she goes at everything she does 100 percent and then some. She writes for the school newspaper. She's the heart and soul of the Shakespeare Club. She's the seventh grade class president. She goes out for public speaking. And that's just what she does at school. On the "outside," she does the occasional modeling gig, throws great parties, rides horses, and is involved in the junior high youth group at church. Her life is full—sometimes too full. At times she dives into things before she really knows what's in store. And sometimes she just doesn't get why the other people in these groups aren't as gung-ho as she is. Lily's solution? Try to do it all—by yourself if you have to—until you drop—or burn out—or just get so disappointed that you quit.

Kresha hangs out with the Girlz, who are a pretty spiritual group. They pray together, often go to church as a group, and for the most part try to figure out what God wants them to do in their lives. Kresha likes everything the Girlz do together, so she goes along with the God thing too. But most of the time, when she's alone, Kresha kind of figures she's got plenty of time to really be a disciple of God's son. She's young now—isn't this the time to have fun and explore her options? When anybody questions her about where she is with God, Kresha's solution is to tell them that her relationship with God is very private—and then go on about her business. But the reality is, she doesn't even have a relationship with God.

Each of our Girlz has a conflict, a tough situation, or a dilemma in some area of her life. Zooey struggles with school. Suzy has issues with sportsmanship. Reni is challenged when it comes to being a leader. Lily gets tangled up in the whole extracurricular activity thing. And Kresha isn't even aware that she's missing out in her relationship with God.

Even though each girl appears to be floundering in a different place, they all have one thing in common. They all need to develop *integrity.*

You may already know what integrity is or you may have heard it enough that you think it has something to do with what lawyers and doctors and judges are supposed to have. They definitely *should* have it— and so should everyone else on the face of the earth!

Integrity is a quality—just as honesty, generosity, and compassion are qualities—that every person needs to develop if she's going to be the *best* she can be at everything she does. Not the best in terms of ability— like Suzy—or natural flair—like Reni—or determination—like Lily. We're talking about being the best *person* you can be. If you have integrity, you can be the best *you* whether you win or lose, fail or succeed, excel or do your best and still barely scrape by.

"Yikes!" you may be saying. "I gotta get me some of that!"

Yes, you do—so let's find out how. We'll start with just exactly what integrity is.

The word itself really means being of sound moral principle, being upright, honest, and sincere. But it comes from a word that means complete, whole, and not easily broken apart.

In case that doesn't exactly clear things up, it might help to see the difference between what it looks like when integrity is missing and when it's a part of you.

NO INTEGRITY

Cop an attitude in class when you don't understand the material.

Take the opportunity to step on the girl on the other team when she trips and falls on the field.

When two of your clubs have meetings at the same time, leave one early and be late to the other one.

As a group leader, don't tell those people who are uncooperative that you're having a meeting. Maybe they'll just quit.

When you're with people who believe in God, say you believe in Him, even though you don't, and when you're with people who don't, make fun of people who do.

LOTS OF INTEGRITY

Admit you're clueless and go to the teacher for help.

Reach down and help her up.

Decide which one you really want to go to and attend that one. Then think it over and decide if you really need to be in both.

Give the people who don't cooperate at meetings a chance to tell you why.

Be honest about how you feel about God and then give Him at least a chance.

You've probably already figured out that integrity is something God wants us to have. Let's take a closer look at that.

HOW IS this a GOD THING?

Time after time, Jesus told the Pharisees — who didn't have a *clue* when it came to integrity — "You are the ones who justify yourselves in the eyes of men, but God knows your hearts" (Luke 16:15).

It's that stuff "behind the appearance" that makes up your integrity. It isn't how smart you are in school — not at all. It's your attitude in class and your drive to do your best, whatever it takes. It isn't how amazing you are at sports. It's how you treat the other players and how you act when the game's over. It isn't how many clubs and activities you're involved in. It's how committed you are and how well you work with the other people who are in the activity with you. It isn't how often you go to church. It's how often you really live the faith you say you believe in.

So — you can be the *best* — even if you don't make straight A's, win first-place trophies, have a different activity going on every day after school, get elected president of every club you join, or get the Sunday school attendance award five years in a row. All it takes is having the integrity to do everything completely and honestly.

In case that's still a little fuzzy around the edges for you, the Bible gives us some good examples.

When Moses was getting burned-out because so many people were coming to him with their problems, his father-in-law Jethro advised him to select some men who could handle the simpler problems on the local level. He told Moses to choose men of integrity, and he spelled out integrity for him. He said that people who have integrity are those who:

- totally respect God.
- can be trusted.
- hate dishonest gain (cheaters, thieves, those kinds of folks).
  (See Exodus 18:21.)

Later, God added some additional pieces to the integrity puzzle. He said people who have integrity:

- don't twist things around to get their way.
- don't accept bribes.
- are always fair. *(See Deuteronomy 16:19–20.)*

Of course, those people back then weren't any quicker than we are, so *years* later, Micah had to tell the people again what God expected in terms of integrity. He said:

"He has showed you, O man, what is good. And what does the LORD require of you?" (Micah 6:8). He said they should:

- act justly.
- love mercy.
- walk humbly with their God.

Centuries later God was still trying to drive the point home through his son Jesus and through his servant John the Baptist. Both talked a lot about integrity. They told the people that:

- the tax collectors should not take any more money from people than they were supposed to (Luke 3:13).
- the soldiers should not blackmail people or accuse them of things they hadn't done (Luke 3:14).
- everyone should treat other people the way they themselves would want to be treated (Luke 6:31).
- they should love their enemies and pray for them (Luke 6:32–36).
- they should not pick on people, jump on their failures, or criticize their faults, but be generous with their blessings (Luke 6:37–38).

Zacchaeus should be praised for his integrity, because he gave half his income to the poor, and if he accidentally cheated anybody, he paid back four times the damages (Luke 19:8).

Jesus took Nathanael on as a disciple because he could tell just by looking at him that he didn't have a false bone in his body (John 1:47).

Finally, the idea of integrity began to stick in people's characters.

When Jesus died, a man named Joseph, who was even a member of the Jewish High Council, took Jesus' instructions so much to heart that he went to Pilate and asked for the body of Jesus. Then he prepared Jesus' body for burial and placed it in the tomb he'd installed for himself. He took a huge risk, but he did it because it was right to do (Luke 23:50–54).

When a man named Simon asked Peter to sell him the apostles' "secret" for healing people, Peter not only refused, he read the guy the riot act for trying to buy God's gift (Acts 8:18–23).

And of course Paul was all *about* integrity. When people started calling Barnabas and him "gods," Paul stopped an entire parade and set them straight, giving God all the credit for the miracles that he and Barnabas had done (Acts 14:12–15). When he was outside of Israel, spreading the gospel, he took up a collection for the poor and brought every cent of it back with him (Acts 24:16–17). When times got hard for him and the rest of the early Christians, he didn't throw up his hands and walk off the job, nor did he try to adjust the message to make it easier so more people would join him. He just told the whole truth and let people judge for themselves (2 Corinthians 4:2).

In fact, the basic quality we have to have if we're going to live Christian lives is integrity. It's the only way, the God way, for you to be the *best you* at everything you do.

✓ Check Yourself Out

Before we talk about *how* you can get this secret ingredient, you need to take a look at where you are right now on the integrity meter. This doesn't mean you're going to find out just how rotten you really are inside! It's just a way for you to figure out where you aren't whole so you can find the right pieces that will *make* you complete.

Circle the letter of the sentence ending that sounds the *most* like what you would do in each situation. Be as *honest* as you can.

1. **If my teacher made a rule that if you got caught chewing gum in class you had to stick it on your nose and leave it there for an hour, I would:**

   a. never chew gum.

   b. be really careful not to get caught when I'm chewing gum.

   c. chew gum on purpose so I can refuse to stick it on my nose.

   d. complain to the teacher about the rule after school.

2. **If my teacher got really sarcastic with people when they messed up doing math problems on the board, I would:**

   a. work hard on my math so I won't mess up.

   b. really hope she doesn't call on me.

   c. be sarcastic right back if she pulls that on me.

   d. ask a grown-up to talk to the teacher about the way she hurts kids' feelings.

3. **If we had a big, important test and I had studied all the wrong stuff, I would:**

   a. tell the teacher I'm sick and can't take the test (which might actually be true when you consider how upset I'd be!).

   b. try to fake my way through it, because what else can I really do?

   c. get mad at the teacher for not being more clear about what was going to be on the test.

   d. do the best I can and write a note on my paper telling the teacher what happened.

4. **If I were working on a group project for school and nobody was getting the job done, I would:**

   a. do it all so I wouldn't get a bad grade.

   b. do my part of the work and hope everybody else gets their act together.

   c. refuse to do any work because I shouldn't have to if nobody else does.

   d. do what I can and try to get the other people to do their parts.

5. **If a class field trip was about to be canceled because somebody took the teacher's CD player, and I knew who did it, I would:**

   a. get the CD player from where they were hiding it and put it back on the teacher's desk when nobody is looking.

   b. figure there is nothing I can do about it.

   c. tell the teacher I don't think it is fair for everybody else to get punished for something one person did.

   d. go to the person who took it and tell her if she doesn't return it I'll have to turn her in.

6. **If I were playing in a soccer game and the referee said I fouled when I didn't, I would:**

   a. be sure to not get anywhere close to the sidelines for the rest of the game.

   b. shrug it off because, after all, it's only a game.

   c. yell at the referee.

d.   make sure the coach knows I didn't make the foul and then let it pass because even referees make mistakes.

7.   **If I were a really good softball player on a team and a friend asked me to go to a hot dog roast on the beach the night I had a practice, I would:**

a.   go to the practice, but resent it the whole time.

b.   tell the coach I can't come to the practice because of family problems and then go to the hot dog roast with my friend.

c.   just not show up for practice. If I'm that good, the coach isn't going to kick me off the team.

d.   ask my friend if she'd invite me next time and then go to practice.

8.   **If a bunch of us in my neighborhood got together everyday after school and practiced on my trampoline in the backyard, and we were getting really good at stunts, I would:**

a.   let a girl who isn't very good at stunts join us, even if it messes things up for the rest of us.

b.   tell a girl who isn't very good at stunts who wants to join us that my parents will only let so many people be around the trampoline at one time.

c.   make fun of a girl that isn't very good at stunts so she'll stop coming.

d.   let a girl who isn't very good at stunts stay with us and try to help her get better.

9.   **If I were in the Drama Club and somebody else got the part in a play that I wanted really badly, I would:**

a.   do an incredible job at the small part I did get so the teacher will wish she'd picked me for the big part.

    b.   do okay at the small part I got and hope the girl who got the role I wanted will get sick or break a leg or something.

    c.   tell everybody the girl who got my part thinks she's all that.

    d.   do a great job with my small part so the whole play will be good.

10. If I'd been taking dance since I was five and I was really tired of it, I would:

    a.   keep taking lessons because my parents have put a lot of money and time into it.

    b.   stop giving it my best and hope the teacher will tell my parents I need to quit.

    c.   flat out tell my parents I plan to quit.

    d.   talk it over with my parents and my dance teacher.

11. If I were president of a club and I had a great idea I wanted the club to do but some people didn't want to do it, I would:

    a.   give up the idea and do what they want to do.

    b.   get together with the people who like my idea and just do it with them.

    c. tell them too bad because I'm the leader so I have the final say.

    d. discuss it with the whole group and see if we can come up with a compromise.

12. If people made fun of me for closing my eyes and saying a silent prayer before I ate my lunch in the school cafeteria, I would:

    a. stop praying before I eat.

    b. pray without closing my eyes or bowing my head.

    c. tell them they aren't going to heaven because *they* don't pray.

    d. ask them to stop—and then silently pray for *them*.

13. If I were at a youth rally and everybody else was really getting into the praise music (waving arms, dancing around, closing their eyes and tilting their faces up) and I wasn't, I would:

    a. pretend I am into it too.

    b. escape to the restroom.

    c. goof around and mimic the people who are into it.

    d. just do what I am moved to do as I sing.

Count how many you circled of each letter and put the numbers in these slots:

"a" _____

"b" _____

"c" _____

"d" _____

Remember that the purpose of checking yourself out is to find out where you are, so you will know what to do to improve your sense of integrity.

Lily and the Creep (Book Three)
Softcover • ISBN 978-0-310-23252-0

Lily learns what it means to be a child of God
and how to develop God's image in herself.

The Buddy Book
Softcover • ISBN 978-0-310-70064-7
(Companion Nonfiction to *Lily and the Creep*)
The Buddy Book is all about relationships—why they're important,
how lousy your life can be if they're crummy, what makes a good
one, and how God is the Counselor for all of them.

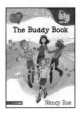

Lily's Ultimate Party (Book Four)
Softcover • ISBN 978-0-310-23253-7

After Lily's plans for the "ultimate" party fall apart, her grandmother shows
Lily that having a party for the right reasons will help to make it a success.

The Best Bash Book
Softcover • ISBN 978-0-310-70065-4
(Companion Nonfiction to *Lily's Ultimate Party*)
The Best Bash Book provides fun party ideas and alternatives,
as well as etiquette for hosting and attending parties.

Ask Lily (Book Five)
Softcover • ISBN 978-0-310-23254-4

Lily becomes the "Answer Girl" and gives
anonymous advice in the school newspaper.

The Blurry Rules Book
Softcover • ISBN 978-0-310-70152-1
(Companion Nonfiction to *Ask Lily*)
Explaining ethics for an 8-12 year old girl! You will discover that although there may
not always be an easy answer or a concrete rule, there's always a God answer.

Available now at your local bookstore!

Lily the Rebel (Book Six)
Softcover • ISBN 978-0-310-23255-1

Lily starts to question the rules at home and at school and decides she may not want to follow the rules.

The It's MY Life Book
Softcover • ISBN 978-0-310-70153-8

(Companion Nonfiction to *Lily the Rebel*)
The It's MY Life Book is designed to help you find balance in your struggle for independence, so you can become not only your best self, but most of all your God-intended self.

Lights, Action, Lily! (Book Seven)
Softcover • ISBN 978-0-310-70249-8

Cast in a Shakespearean play at school by a mere fluke, Lily is immediately convinced she's destined for a career on Broadway, but finally learns through a series of entanglements that relationships are more important than a perfect performance.

The Creativity Book
Softcover • ISBN 978-0-310-70247-4

(Companion Nonfiction to *Lights, Action, Lily!*)
Discover your creativity and learn to enjoy the arts in this fun, activity-filled book written by Nancy Rue.

Lily Rules! (Book Eight)
Softcover • ISBN 978-0-310-70250-4

Lily is voted class president at her school, but unlike her predecessors who have been content to sail along with the title and a picture in the yearbook, Lily is out to make changes.

The Uniquely Me Book
Softcover • ISBN 978-0-310-70248-1

(Companion Nonfiction to *Lily Rules!*)
At some point, every girl wonders why she was born and why she's the way she is. Well, author Nancy Rue has written the perfect book designed to answer all those nagging uncertainties from a biblical perspective.

Rough & Rugged Lily (Book Nine)
Softcover • ISBN 978-0-310-70260-3

Lily's convinced she's destined to become a great outdoorswoman, but when the Robbins family is stranded in a snowstorm on the way to a mountain cabin to celebrate Christmas, she learns the real meaning of survival and how dependent she is on the material things of life.

The Year 'Round Holiday Book
Softcover • ISBN 978-0-310-70256-6

(Companion Nonfiction to *Rough and Rugged Lily*)
The Year 'Round Holiday Book will help you celebrate traditional holidays with not only fun and pizzazz, but with deeper meaning as well.

Lily Speaks! (Book Ten)
Softcover • ISBN 978-0-310-70262-7

Lily enters the big speech contest at school and learns the up and downsides of competition through her pain and disappointment, as well as the surprise benefits, and how God heals jealousy, envy, and self-doubt.

The Values & Virtues Book
Softcover • ISBN 978-0-310-70257-3

(Companion Nonfiction to *Lily Speaks!*)
The Values & Virtues Book offers you tips and skills for improving your study habits, sportsmanship, relationships, and every area of your life.

Available now at your local bookstore!

Horse Crazy Lily (Book Eleven)
Softcover • ISBN 978-0-310-70263-4

Lily's in love! With horses?! Back in the "saddle" for another exciting adventure, Lily's gone western and feels she's destined to be the next famous cowgirl.

The Fun-Finder Book
Softcover • ISBN 978-0-310-70258-0

(Companion Nonfiction to *Horse Crazy Lily*)

The Fun-Finder Book is designed to help you find out what you like so that you can develop your own just-for-you hobby. And if you just can't figure it out, a self-quiz helps you recognize your likes and dislikes as you discover your God-given talent.

Lily's Church Camp Adventure (Book Twelve)
Softcover • ISBN 978-0-310-70264-1

Lily learns a real lesson about the essential habits of the heart when she and the Girlz attend Camp Galilee.

The Walk-the-Walk Book
Softcover • ISBN 978-0-310-70259-7

(Companion Nonfiction to *Lily's Church Camp Adventure*)

Every young girl needs the training that develops positive and lifelong spiritual habits. Prayer, Bible study, devotion, simplicity, confession, worship, and celebration are foundational spiritual disciplines to help you "walk-the-walk."

Lily's in London?! (Book Thirteen)
Softcover • ISBN 978-0-310-70554-3

Lily's London adventures strengthen her relationship with God as she realizes, more than ever, there are many possibilities for walking her spiritual path in Christ.

Lily's Passport to Paris (Book Fourteen)
Softcover • ISBN 978-0-310-70555-0

Lily visits Paris and meets Christophe, an orphan boy at the mission where her mom is working. While helping Christophe to understand who God is, Lily finally discovers her own mission. This last book in the series also includes a letter from Nancy Rue, which tells what happens to the characters after the series ends, and introduces the character of Sophie LaCroix from the Faithgirlz! Sophie Series.

Available now at your local bookstore!

faiThGirLz!
the beauty of believing

A Lucy Novel
Written by Nancy Rue

New from Faithgirlz! By bestselling author Nancy Rue.

Lucy Rooney is a feisty, precocious tomboy who questions everything—even God. It's not hard to see why: a horrible accident killed her mother and blinded her father, turning her life upside down. It will take a strong but gentle housekeeper—who insists on Bible study and homework when all Lucy wants to do is play soccer—to show Lucy that there are many ways to become the woman God intends her to be.

Book 1: Lucy Doesn't Wear Pink
ISBN 9780310714507

Book 2: Lucy Out of Bounds
ISBN 9780310714514

Book 3: Lucy's Perfect Summer
ISBN 9780310714521 Available May 2009!

Book 4: Lucy Finds Her Way
ISBN 9780310714538 Available August 2009!

Available now at your local bookstore!
Visit www.faithgirlz.com, it's the place for girls ages 9-12.

NIV Young Women of Faith Bible

General Editor: Susie Shellenberger

Hardcover • ISBN 978-0-310-91394-8

Softcover • ISBN 978-0-310-70278-8

Now there is a study Bible designed especially for
girls ages 8 to 12. Created to develop a habit of studying God's
Word in young girls, the *NIV Young Women of Faith Bible* is full of
cool, fun to read in-text features that are not only interesting, but
provide insight. It has 52 weekly studies thematically tied to the
NIV Women of Faith Study Bible to encourage a special time of
study for mothers and daughters to share in God's Word.

Available now at your local bookstore!